Readers of ***A Slice Life***

"Hansen observes the human condition with an economy of words, precise and well-chosen. As a reader, you interact with her stories, feeling the humor or despair or unanswered question exactly when and where she wants. Her settings and characters are often mundane but her messages profound." — Linda B. Myers

"These stories grab me and pull me right in. I find myself wondering about the character later, and have to remind myself, oh yes it was just a story." — Darcy Hansen Harris

"Hansen lifts comic moments up and takes us on a ride into lives of sincere, hardworking families. Every story is relevant and timeless. The characters are people you want to know. They make poor choices, get into trouble, get bullied, become confused and decide to make right what has gone wrong. These stories will stay with you. She pulls us into a quirky, tender, wonderful world and we don't want to leave. Her story telling reminds me of Eudora Welty and O. Henry. If you enjoyed "Olive Kitteridge," you will love these stories." — Teya Priest Johnston

"Hansen's stories engage me every time. Plenty of action, humor, believable characters and quirky, real-life situations. She knows how to engage her readers. You won't be able to read just one without wanting to read more." — R. Marcus

"Hansen's stories are funny, funnier and the funniest - she will make you laugh. Whether you have ever worked in a call center or had an obsession with shoes you will recognize and laugh with these characters." — J. Duncan

"Hansen's delightful short stories are filled with characters that remind readers of their own friends, family members and neighbors. Her vivid imagery and clear, succient prose, fill her stories with "laugh out loud" humor, surprising twists, compassion and sometimes a haunting insight." — Donna Downes

A Slice Of Life

Collected Stories

By Heidi Hansen

H3 Press
2016

First Printing: 2016

ISBN 978-0-9982526-0-5

Published by:
H3 Press, PO Box 312, Carlsborg, WA 98324
H3Press@olypen.com

Dedication

This book is dedicated to my family:
my four sons, my six sisters, Alan,
and to my fellow writers
who have written with me,
listened to my stories,
and provided encouragement and
guidance along the way.

Contents

Let There Be Cake

Did you bake a cake?" My mother's question floated up the stairs into my room where I lay reading Nancy Drew and "The Secret of the Old Clock."

"Did. You. Bake A Cake?" Her voice barked out each word. I wondered who she was talking to, and set the book down to listen.

"DID YOU BAKE A CAKE? A CAKE?" I realized she was on the phone with my grandmother. She is hard of hearing and stubborn.

"Who's mom yelling at?" my sister Katie asked, as she came into my room.

"She's on the phone with grandma," I said.

"Oh." She sat down at the foot of my bed.

I picked up the book, going back to the mystery.

"Do you want to go bake a cake?" Katie asked.

"What?" I shouted annoyed because I was rereading the same paragraph again.

"Did you bake a cake? You said you might," mother said.

"Maybe mom wants cake. We could go make one," Katie said.

"What kind?" I couldn't believe I said that. I wanted to read.

"Chocolate," Katie said.

"Hmmm." I was still trying to get over why I asked that question.

"Okay. Do you want pineapple upside down?"

"WHAT?" Mom's voice boomed. It startled us. I sat up, and the book clattered to the floor. Katie and I looked at each other, the way kids do when they know something important is happening. Without a word, we tiptoed from the bedroom to listen in the hall.

We heard mom say, "No one stole your dresses."

"Is she still talking to Grandma?" Katie whispered.

I hunched my shoulders in response but kept listening. We couldn't hear anything for a moment. We moved to the top of the stairwell.

I'll see you tomorrow." Mom said. The receiver clanked into the cradle.

Dad asked, "What's going on?"

"I called to make sure she was okay and asked if she had baked a cake. She didn't hear me and kept talking about a robbery. Finally, I was able to understand that when she went to her closet, she found all of her dresses missing. She kept asking, 'why would anyone want to steal my dresses?'"

"Do we need to call the police?" dad said.

Katie and I looked at each other exchanging huge eyes. She came closer and leaned against me. Was our grandmother the victim of a robbery?

"No. I noticed that her dress was stained today, and realized she doesn't see this anymore. When I looked over her other garments, I found them in the same condition, so I brought them home to launder them. She was with me when I took them."

"So she knew you took them?"

"Yes, she forgot, I guess."

There was a silence between my parents that was more than the lack of voices. I couldn't understand it then, but I felt it.

"So?" Katie said.

"So what?" I wanted to get back to my Nancy Drew mystery.

"Let's bake a cake," she said.

I wanted my solitary reading, but now the thought of cake was compelling.

"Chocolate," I said.

"Chocolate frosting, too," she said.

We galloped down the wooden steps. The sound reverberated through the old farmhouse.

"Stop running in the house," Dad called out.

"What are you girls up to? Mom asked.

"We're gonna' bake a cake."

Hot August Night

Cletus rode the fence line along the northern boundary across his one hundred acres. It was late August. The crops were in, the hay baled and stowed in the barn for the winter. Rains were expected soon, then snow. Fences needed to be mended now.

He tied bits of orange ribbon to indicate where repairs were needed and noted the posts to be replaced. When he reached the eastern corner, he sat down and ate the sandwiches he had packed. He had to move along to the south, then west, then north, back home. This was lonesome work, might take him more than one day. Not that Cletus had much more than lonely days and nights. He sighed thinking about what he had once dreamt for himself. He had wanted to travel, see the world, explore. As a boy he had envisioned the hayloft as Mt. Everest and he alone could climb it. When he jumped into the pond on a hot summer day, he imagined that he was swimming across the English Channel. Yet here he was, still on the family farm, tied to it as his father had been. He had never been further than a hundred miles from it.

He drove the thirty-seven miles into town in his battered pickup and ordered the posts and a spool of wire to do the mending. At dusk, he called in the two cows and three horses and shut the barn doors for the night. There were storm warnings and the wind shifted. He sat down at the kitchen table. Mary Alice set a plate of stew, steaming hot, in front of him. He grunted an acknowledgment. He meant it as thanks.

"Best I can do with what we got," she snarled, thinking he was registering his disgust at the leftovers. She stormed out of the kitchen.

Cletus stared after her not understanding her fury. They didn't communicate well. He stabbed a large chunk of beef and brought it to his mouth. He heard the cows low and the horses snort, then he heard a sound he could not identify. Was it the wind? Not sure what that noise was, he laid the fork down. He jerked open the door and stood on the wide porch looking across the yard to where the barn stood. Low clouds blotted the moon. He heard nothing more. Hunger beat curiosity.

He went back to the table and reclaimed the food. He got two bites in when he heard the noise again. The horses stamped their hooves in terror. "What the hell?" he said, scraping back the chair. The fork clanked against the plate, and the milk in the glass sloshed over the rim.

At the door, he grabbed the lantern and struck a match along the doorjamb, lighting the lantern as he crossed the porch. The barn doors were shut. The air was still and warm. Weather reports had said a storm was expected, cold wind, and rain. This did not feel like a storm. It felt clammy, warm, and damp. There was a singed hair smell in the air like something had burned, but there was no smoke. Had something been in the barn when he had fed the livestock earlier? He opened the door and stepped inside. He reached for the shotgun he kept there on the wall.

What he saw made him stop. The lantern fell to the barn floor. He shook his head as if to clear the image, rubbed his eyes, blinked, and looked again

A spherical machine filled the interior of the barn. It was dull gunmetal gray, and there was a glow from it though no individual lights could be seen. There were no other words to describe it other than... Cletus was hesitant to think them. It was a flying saucer, a UFO. How did anything so big get into the barn? He looked up and saw that the roof of the barn was gone and stars glittered in the night sky. He whistled for the horses, but there was no response. He did not hear the cows. Had the aliens killed his animals? Why was a spaceship here?

He stood maybe twelve feet from the machine, and he wanted to touch it. He took two steps forward and waited for a sign. Getting none, he took two long strides to close the distance. He stretched out his left hand and ran it over the cold, smooth metal. It was without any signs of manufacture, no rivets or seams. He looked up, tried to estimate the height. It went nearly all the way to the roof; the hayloft was gone. Suddenly there was a high-pitched sound that made him cover his ears. It was piercing, and he turned away.

He wasn't sure what happened next. Mary Alice screamed and dragged him out of the burning barn. The entire building was engulfed in flames; the heat intense, the rafters fell inward into a heap. It looked like a huge bonfire but only for him and Mary Alice.

"What happened?" he asked. The sun was rising. He had lost most of the night.

"It was the lantern," she said. "Whatever were you doing in the barn?"

"I...we heard the horses. I went to see what was in the barn. You remember hearing that don't you?"

She looked at him with a cocked eye. "Cletus, you ate dinner and went out on the porch. That's what I heard."

Cletus sat on the porch looking at the glowing pile of embers that had been the barn. There was no sign of the horses or cows. A winter's worth of hay was gone, too.

He sighed. He didn't want to be one of those people who told their UFO experience and then was labeled a weirdo, but that was what he had seen. The fire might have started when he dropped the lantern, but the aliens might have burned it down when they started up their engines. They could have killed him. They could have taken him into their spaceship and off to their far distant planet.

He looked at Mary Alice who was still blabbering about him burning down the barn, and what he should be doing, and how this was going to set them back. He knew she wouldn't listen if he tried to tell her about the flying saucer. He hung his head. Why hadn't they taken him?

In The Park

I arrive early; she will be late, as usual. I am to meet my daughter-in-law, Marsha, and two grandsons today. I sit on the bench in the park watching the children on the playground. They climb the slide, down, up, down again. On the swings swinging to and fro, to and fro. A small boy bounces a bright blue ball. Bouncing it higher than he can reach, racing forward to catch it as it falls. When the ball rises, I see that it matches the cloudless sky. He progresses across the playground in this manner.

I tap my watch irritated by her tardiness.

"Stop!" A child's screech brings everything to a standstill. Only the squeak squeak of the chains on the swings can be heard.

"Stop!" he shouts again.

I turn to the source of the scream and see the boy who was bouncing the blue ball. He doesn't have the ball anymore. Two much older and larger boys have taken the ball and repeatedly toss the ball back and forth over the younger boy's head. Each time it flies over him, he raises his arms and lifts his body to intercept it. Each time he fails to capture it, he yells, "Stop!"

After many times, his voice weakens, and he begins to cry. The older boys may have tired of the teasing, but this re-energizes them. They jump about and toss the ball menacingly close behind the smaller boy.

Are the boys playing? Are they just being boys? Or are they sinister? Cruel? Thieves in training? Should I intervene? I surely would if my grandsons were the targets of this taunt.

Witnessing this, I drift back to a time in my youth. In the blink of an eye, tears well, one slipping down my cheek. I was the receiver in a similar incident. I don't remember all the details, but I remember the pain. We had moved and making new friends was difficult. My mother quickly became friends with another woman. They each had five daughters, which seemed to cement their relationship.

Of course, her five and our five overlapped in age, and there were several of us that were the same age. My mother encouraged me over and over again to become friends with Mary, my redheaded counterpart. That first summer there were several attempts to bring us together, an outing in the park, a trip to the public pool. While I tried to strike up a friendship, she didn't show any interest.

When school started, it was apparent that she was the center of the clique of the most popular girls. I was on the outside; too shy to break through. There was no connection between us.

Imagine my surprise when Mary called one day to invite me to a sleep over. It would be the three of us, Mary, Vickie, and myself. I didn't question why the most popular girls in school were asking me to join in. I asked my mother for permission and to drive me over. I packed my pajamas and toothbrush.

I can't recall if I was between fourth and fifth or between fifth and sixth grade, but I remember my mother dropping me off. I bounded out of the car and up to the front door. Vickie's mother was kneeling in the flowerbeds. She smiled and said to go inside. I saw Vickie and Mary down the hall. As I approached them, they closed the door and giggled. I stood in the hall, alone. I knocked, they laughed. I waited. I knocked again. And again.

After a while they opened the door, I took a step toward the room, but they slammed the door and laughed. That was repeated. I was moving from concern to frustration. Why did they invite me if this is how they were treating me? I did not understand what was going on. Maybe it was a game like "Hide and Seek," but I didn't know it.

The game changed. Mary opened the door and let me in. I sat down, they jumped up and ran out. The girls giggled as they darted from one room to another. As I entered a room, they left. They moved to the garage. I followed them. They climbed into the car and locked all the doors. Remember when each door had a stem you had to push down to lock the door? You had to pull it up to unlock the door.

Inside the car, they taunted me, jumping from seat to seat. They'd unlock a door on one side of the car, and entice me to come in; as I'd reach the door, they'd lock it. And laugh.

"Come on, come over here. It's unlocked."

I hurried over and reached for the handle. Looking at me, they locked that door. "Sorry, come over here. This is unlocked. Hurry."

This went on for some time. Time enough for me to realize that this was their game. I didn't have to play. I had a choice. I turned from the car, marched back into the house, lifted the receiver on the hall phone and called my mother.

How long had it been since she dropped me off? It was at least a fifteen-minute drive from home. Had she returned? Did she go somewhere else?

She answered the phone, and I sobbed. Somehow I was able to bleat out "come and get me."

"What's the matter? Are you alright?" She sounded worried.

"Come and get me now," I said.

All these years later, I wonder why they invited me. Had they planned to tease me? Or had this been a bit of innocent mischief?

I see Marsha's car pull into the lot across the park. I wipe away the tears and jog over to where the boy cries. I see Isaac and Michael running to meet me. I reach out and snatch the ball, catching it before it falls into the hands of one of the teasers. I offer it to the small boy.

"Come play near me. Here come my grandsons." I tell him.

"Shame on you," I say to each of the older boys. "Shame on you."

"Michael. Isaac." I call, embracing them as they reach me. "Let's play."

"Sorry we're late," Marsha said.

"Oh no, not late, perfect," I said.

Dreams

I slept last night. The first real slumber in months. I plunged into it, tumbled down the rabbit hole, deep, deep into the earth, cocooned and swaddled in a warm nest. I slept.

I found myself the center of attention. Wherever I was, whatever was happening, people clamored to be near me. Hands outreached, stretching toward me, hundreds of faces smiling. I extended my hand to embrace theirs, then the scene slanted. They demanded money.

"Put it to use, man!" a longhaired youth in jeans shouted.

"Feed the poor," a woman dressed in rags said to me.

A young woman in a wheelchair murmured, "Imagine who you could help."

Their words swirled as they shouted. I felt coins in the pockets of my pants, and I reached in. What tumbled out were hundred dollar bills, handfuls of them. I pressed them into every hand, but they continued to fall out, piling up at my feet. What was all this money? A crowd formed, kneeling and plucking it up. When there was no more, they tore at my pockets and clothing. "Give me...give me...give me."

"You need to be more careful," a bespectacled man said. He morphed into the Monopoly Man as he swaggered away in his top hat, with his cane.

Next, I was in a tall office building, overlooking the city. The room was large with windows all around; I could see birds in flight and planes on the horizon. The table was as long as the room, in every chair sat a man in a suit. They all looked the same, exactly the same, dark blue suit, white shirt, red tie, hair short, slicked back, steel gray glasses on the bridges of their noses. Each man was talking, tapping at graphs. When these men spoke, numbers tumbled out of their mouths and hung in the air. Every number had a dollar sign in front and lots of zeroes and commas afterward. I could not hear them speak, I only saw the numbers. Then the graphs snapped themselves shut like window shades, and the room disappeared.

Alone in dim light, I smelled the aroma of my Grandmother's minestrone. "Nana," I called out in my child voice. There was no response. I came upon a large bubbling black cauldron. I was hungry and looked into it. There was no soup, only gold bullion. I turned to run calling out, "Nana, Nana."

Around me were shelves filled with long metal boxes that required two keys to open. I searched my pockets and found them now full of keys but did not know which key went to which box. I was ravenous and used the keys to open the boxes. Each box was filled with dollar bills, stock certificates, and gold coins, but no food.

On the floor, a newspaper with my picture on the front page read, "W. Harrison Groves, heir to the Groves fortune purported to be worth over five hundred billion dollars." My photo was on every page of the newspaper.

A desperate feeling came over me, I had to get out of the room. There was only one door, a heavy metal door with no handle. I pounded on the door.

Around me was nothing but money. The stench of it made me retch. From within me came more gold coins, gold coins littered the floor. I threw up more and more.

I heard a phone ringing in the distance. Perhaps this was help. At each ring, it multiplied over and over until it was a continual cacophony of ringing bells. No phone in sight. I slammed my palms over my ears to shut it out.

I wake to the shrill whistle in the train yard. I blink at the sunlight dancing on the bedroom wall and twist to look at the bedside clock. It is just after seven o'clock. Where was the alarm? I swing my legs over the bed and scuffle off to the bathroom. The dog has been drinking from the toilet, my bare feet find droplets of water on the floor. I wash my face and hands and look at my reflection. What was that dream I had last night?

I walk the dog before I leave for work. I am happy to be back on the day shift; three years of night shift was too long, too lonely. Perhaps now I can meet my neighbors and have more of a social life, start to date again. I ride the subway to my post where I collect tolls on the bridge.

Everyone hurries. I see panhandlers on the street corners and men in suits walking by without a glance. Their hands are in their pockets. The dream comes back to me, and I remember what my hands found then. I used to watch people and imagine stories about their lives.

I used to daydream what it would be like to be the person in the back seat of the long black limo as it crossed the bridge. Now, I shudder at the thought.

The Skier

Liz slouched in the chair, her left leg ached, she blamed it on skiing the day before. That day started at daybreak, and she had practiced the downhill runs till sundown, mastering the moguls, and increasing her speed through the gates. Her knee screamed in agony, Liz bit her lower lip. "This is the price an athlete has to pay," she heard her coach's words echo. Tomorrow, it will be better after physical therapy. She sat in the green waiting room beside all the dated magazines waiting for physical therapy.

A woman with graying hair sat beside her; there was something familiar about the woman, but they had not spoken. She wondered why the woman took the seat right next to her when there were plenty of other seats available. She didn't ask, and the other woman had her nose in a magazine. Liz pulled her purse closer to her body to be safe.

The nurse appeared dressed in colorful cotton pajamas, at least that is what they looked like. She called out a name and looked around the room. One man rose slowly from his chair, leaning on his cane, then shuffled toward the nurse. She escorted him down the hall, the door closed behind them. Liz glanced at her watch and wondered why this was taking so long.

"Stop fidgeting," said the woman beside her.

"Excuse me?" Liz said.

"We were early," she said.

"How would you know?"

Liz watched as the gray-haired woman resituated her body in the chair, and took up another magazine. Perhaps this woman was someone who had lost her memory and had confused Liz for someone she knew. Yes, of course, that must be it. Be kind, she told herself. Someday that could be me.

The nurse appeared again and called out, "Liz McVay."

Liz leaned heavily on the arm of the chair to lift herself keeping the weight off her left leg as much as possible. "Ooooooh," escaped her lips despite her resolve.

"Let me help you," said the woman beside her.

"I'm fine. I can do it myself," Liz said. "Thank you, though."

As Liz approached the nurse, she realized that the woman was still trailing her. The pain in her knee distracted her. Sitting so long only made the pain worse now that she was trying to walk again. She should have iced it before coming in for physical therapy she thought, pushing aside the question of who the woman was. She would let the nurse handle the situation from here.

"Good afternoon Liz," she said. "Looks like you're still having some problem with your leg. Doesn't look any less painful than last week."

"Last week? I only hurt it yesterday," Liz said. Why do these people always mix me up with someone else? No wonder doctors amputate the wrong leg. No one pays attention anymore.

"She's not with us today," said the gray-haired woman.

"I'm sorry to hear that," said the nurse.

Liz looked from one to the other, and tsk'd her teeth. She wondered who they were talking about, and why they weren't paying attention to her. It was all very confusing.

The nurse opened the door to the examination room and motioned for Liz to take a seat on the table.

"This isn't physical therapy," Liz said.

"No, it's your checkup. Dr. Jackson will be in shortly to examine your leg."

"No. No. No," Liz said. "I'm not here for an exam. I'm here for physical therapy. I'm the skier. I'm in training. My coach set up this appointment."

The nurse looked from Liz to the woman and back again. She seemed confused. "Please, have a seat," she said, closing the door.

"Who are you?" Liz asked the woman. "We haven't been introduced, and I don't know why you are here with me at physical therapy."

"Mom, I'm your daughter, Rose."

"Daughter? How old do you think I am? You are confused. I'm twenty-two. You are an old woman. You think I am your daughter?"

"No. Mom. Sit. Be calm. We'll be home soon."

"Home? I've got practice this afternoon. We just need to get my knee working again. I've got prelims on Saturday."

"You won the gold medal."

"I what?"

"You won, Mom. You got the gold medal in the giant slalom. You fell the next year. It has bothered you the rest of your life."

"Are you a fortune teller?"

The woman looked at Liz. Liz stared back at her. Even a stranger would recognize it as the same face looking from one to the other; the only difference is the twenty-four years between. They have shared their lives for forty-eight years, but only Rose has access to those memories. Liz was lost in the thrill of the race for the gold medal, a race she spent twenty-two years preparing for, a race she skied more than fifty years ago.

Liz laid back on the exam table puzzling over what the woman said. Sleep came easy, but only for a short time.

"Where am I?" she questioned in a frail voice.

"We're at the doctors," Rose said.

"Are we done?"

"Not yet."

"Why does it take so long?"

"They have to refit the prosthesis, Mom. You know it takes time."

"I'm tired."

"You had a little nap."

"I did? I'm hungry."

"Want to try that new deli on the way home?"

"Can we just get take out? My leg is all itchy, and it hurts." Liz removed the sheet that lay across her lap. She reached down to scratch her left leg. Her right leg lay on the exam table, nothing dangling from her left hip.

"Damn! I forget sometimes. It feels like it's still there."

"I know that feeling, Mom. It's nice to have you here for a moment."

"It's always a good day when I see you, Rose. You sure look good."

The Struggle

Violet McKenzie leaned back in her seat and took her husband's hand as the train left the station. Violet was struggling with right and wrong. She knew the difference and had done wrong.

"It'll be a great vacation," he said squeezing her hand.

"I love you, Henry," she said.

The train passed through familiar neighborhoods. It would take another half hour of frequent stops before they would get up to speed. Violet closed her eyes and wished this to be the beginning of happiness. She heard the familiar sound, the slight flap of his lips as he exhaled through his mouth that signaled he was asleep. After twenty-three years of marriage, she wondered about secrets they kept from each other. She knew what she had done.

She hadn't intended on the affair. It started with a simple flirtation in a ceramics class. She had always wanted to throw a pot on a wheel. He had been the other older student, and they had laughed at their lopsided creations while the younger students seemed to be artisans. Laughing had led to coffee, then one of them had opened the door and shared some inner truth. That is what she missed with Henry. She didn't know what was going on with his work or among his closest friends. Everything between them felt on the surface, not deep-rooted as it had been. And then, she knew what Jack was thinking, what was going on his life. He knew what she was thinking, what she needed, wanted, and he kept saying and doing those things that made her smile. It was easy to touch him, let him touch her. Suddenly they were planning weekend escapes, and Henry hardly noticed. He didn't question her plan to visit the wine country with an imaginary girlfriend or a shopping trip to New York. He didn't ask about what she bought or did she see a show. He kissed her goodbye and hello, and life went on.

Henry stirred in his sleep and grumbled as if reacting to her thoughts. She tried to think quieter. She still held his hand, he squeezed it now and then and settled back into a soft snore. The last thing she wanted was to hurt Henry or to end their marriage. She marveled at the idiocy of her thought. She had a love affair with another man but didn't want to end her marriage or hurt her husband. What had she wanted? Some attention? To be in the spotlight one more time before she admitted she was old? Perhaps she told herself, that was all it was. Selfish me.

She dropped Henry's hand, wrapping her arms around herself not in an embrace of love, but of disgust and fear. She would still be playing around with Jack if not for the demands he began to make. How long did it take before he wanted more than she was willing to give? When they were in Napa, it was perfect. When they were in New York, it began to be less perfect. First, she had caught him going through her purse. Then she had found him taking photos of her while she slept.

"What? What are you doing?"

Not to worry, they're just for me. I love you so much," he said.

Even as he said this, she felt a chill. She tried to forget it in their lovemaking, but there was a bubble of doubt floating around. As her concerns multiplied, she began to face reality. Why was Jack so enamored with her? She was a married, middle-aged woman with no future for them. Why was this enough for him? Why was it enough for her? What kind of a monster was she? If not a monster, surely a fool.

One night, Henry walked in the front door, and the phone rang. She answered the phone.

"Did I catch you at a bad time?" Jack whispered.

"Can't talk now," she said and hung up.

"What's for dinner tonight? Wanna' go out?" Henry asked.

"I've got dinner in the oven, chicken pot pie," she said, then turned away and replayed what had happened. Jack had never called her on her home phone, they always used their cell phones. She was careful to remove his voicemails and delete the history should Henry look at her phone, but he did not. Why had Jack whispered like that? Why did he start with "did I catch you at a bad time," as if he knew that Henry had just walked in? Was he watching her house? She picked up the phone and checked the caller id. It was his cell phone number. He could be sitting outside.

All this made her heart ache and her nerves raw. She hated herself for what she had done. It wasn't just that she had been unfaithful to Henry, but also that she had violated her own values. I have whored myself for a little attention she thought.

She turned and looked at Henry as he slept. Did he know? Did he have any idea? Would Jack contact him and tell him, show him the photos, make him realize that this had been going on? If he did, how would Henry react?

She closed her eyes as if to stop the painful introspection. I need to put this behind me. Will Jack let me go quietly?

She called it quits after that phone call. Just as their relationship had begun when they developed trust, it was over when that trust was broken. He cried and said that he hadn't meant to call her at home, but she wasn't answering her cell phone, and he was missing her. She had pulled out her cell phone, buried in her purse, and there were two calls. She could never be sure if they came before the phone rang in the house or after she hung up.

He followed her the next week when she went out, so he was watching her. He would show up sauntering down the aisle in the grocery store.

"Oh, Hi Violet. Long time, no see."

"Imagine seeing you here," he said when she had gone to the pottery shop to pick up her last project. He was there, but he had no pieces to fire or retrieve. He was just there.

The last time she saw Jack was when she had gone to meet Henry at his office. When she walked into the lobby, Jack was standing there at the reception desk staring at her. That was the last straw. She had called him and said that he was not to contact her again or to follow her.

"Don't make me get a restraining order, Jack," she said.

"Or what? You're going to huff and puff and blow me away?" He laughed at her and hung up.

Then she did what she should have done at the beginning. She went online and researched him. There were numerous reports from women that he had stalked them and disobeyed their restraining orders.

Henry said, "Honey you seem a little tense, what's bothering you?"

"Perhaps a week away in the country," she said.

"That's a good idea." She thought he meant for her to go alone or with a girlfriend, but then he said, "Let's go next week. I can take a break too."

She fell back in love with him. There was nothing being held back but the ugly affair, and she was pedaling as fast as she could to put it behind her.

Henry stirred again and woke.

"Guess I needed that nap. Now I need the bathroom." He rose and ambled down the car.

Violet exhaled trying to relieve the tension. She wanted to enjoy the trip. A hand touched her shoulder, and she jumped. She turned assuming it was Henry, only to find Jack leering at her.

"What? What are you doing here?" she sputtered.

"I'm missing you, sweetie," he said with a grin. "Follow me up to the next car."

"No. We're through. Go," she said.

"We're in love," he said. "C'mon, we've got time for a quickie."

She wondered if the couple in front of her heard him. Henry would be back shortly. She steeled herself not to turn and look over her shoulder. She looked down at her feet, she would not look at Jack.

"Have it your way. You'll regret it," he said. He walked toward the forward car.

After lunch, she fell asleep with her head on Henry's shoulder. He was reading a digital book, and the rhythm of the train quickly lulled her to sleep. When she woke, Henry was snoring, and it was dark outside. As she returned to consciousness, she realized that Jack stood at the car entrance staring at her. She wondered if his stare had awakened her. She glared at him. He opened the car door and stepped out onto the platform. She followed. He walked through the next car and onto the platform. She followed, stopping there to confront him. He grabbed her shoulders and shook her, then pulled her close, held her firmly.

"You're not going to do this to me," he snarled.

"It's over Jack. Let me go."

"I'm not going to do that. You can't get rid of me."

"Stop. Let me go." She struggled to get out of his grasp. She could wiggle free from one hand but not both. She put her foot behind his, trying to trip him. He pushed her against the railing between the cars. She could see through the grating to the tracks below. She could feel the rush of air.

"Stop fighting me! If you won't leave him, then you'll have to...."

Violet raised her knee and caught him in the groin. He doubled over in pain and in that second she backed out of his grasp. She looked into the car ahead and saw no one looking back at her. She turned her head to look into the car behind for help, but Jack propelled himself toward her, his arms outstretched to grab her.

"You bitch! Just like all the bitches."

She jumped across the platform away from him as he fell on the spot where she had stood. He lunged toward her again but lost his footing and fell forward off the platform into the night.

There was a sound like "Oooff." Then there was only the sound of the train on the track. Violet stood there looking over the edge wondering what to do. She stepped back into the car and into the restroom. She splashed cold water on her face, washed her hands and stared at the blank eyes in the mirror. She weighed the question of reporting a man overboard or not.

Realizing it may be too late, she walked back through the car and took her seat.

As the train slowed coming into the station, Henry said, "Violet, wake up, we're here."

Family Fun

It's June, and the family has gathered for our annual picnic at which someone will draw the card that names them as host for the Thanksgiving Holiday dinner.

I've drawn that card the previous three years. That's three years in a row. When I complain, they all compliment me saying what a marvelous job I have done, how the turkey was cooked just so, and the vegetables are farm fresh and the pies. They go on and on about the pies. There is no way that I will draw that card again this year. What are the odds?

They never seem to want to pitch in or help out. Knowing I live in the country, raise my own poultry, and keep a vegetable garden seems to make it natural for me to want to host this annual dinner.

I sit back and watch as they shuffle the cards and place them in a blue plastic sand bucket. My brother and his wife are hosting the picnic. They had it catered in their backyard. The kids are splashing in the pool; drinks are in our hands when the drawing begins. They pass the bucket, everyone snickers and jokes. The family includes my brother, my two sisters, my aunt and uncle, three cousins, and a couple of close friends that we have claimed as family. Of course, the dinner also includes our maiden aunts, but being in their eighties, we would never expect them to host the dinner. With the kids, it is a banquet for twenty-seven.

As they pass the bucket around the patio, I watch as one by one they reach in, pull out a card, and read, "Not this year." I am the second to last to draw, which I don't find very fair. Having hosted the previous three years, I should be first at least. I push my hand down into the bucket. There are only two cards left. I pluck one, then the other. Indecision sets in. "Pick one," I command my hand. I pull out the card, flip it over and before I can read it, my cousin Carol grabs the last card and reads, "Not this year." I look at the card in my hand, "Host."

"Again?"

"Unbelievable sis," my brother said. "Who's ready for another beer?"

As the party breaks up, I take a garbage bag and start clearing the patio area. Among the plates of partially eaten chicken and potato salad, I see a card. I pick it up and place it in my pocket. I assume we use the same cards each year. By the end of the clean up, I have accumulated six or seven cards. I intend to give them back to my brother, but I forget.

At home, I take off my shorts and find the cards in the pocket. I glance at the cards as I set them on the table and realize that each card reads, "Host." My brother Frank has been the architect of this little trick. Rather than ask me to host, they have concocted this ruse making me think I have picked the only "Host" card. In truth, all the cards read "Host." I realize that they shout out, "Not this year," and that is not what is on the cards.

I pick up the phone to demand an explanation, then hang up knowing that there is a better way to even the score.

Frank works in insurance, and he is one of those people who can work all day with actuary tables and calculate statistics. I wait about a week, and then I call him.

"Hey, brother, those calculators of yours working?"

"Yeah. What's up?"

"I was telling someone about the fact that four years in a row I've drawn the host card and what are those odds?"

"Well...."

"A guy I know at the bank says that it sounds to him like I am on a lucky streak. "Really?" I say, and he says "Sure," and tells me some story about someone who bought a lot of lottery tickets."

"Jeez sis, you are not taking this serious are you?"

"Well, I was thinking. I've never been lucky before, maybe this is my time. Maybe there is something to this. Maybe this is my chance."

"Sis, seriously don't."

"Look it wasn't that bad. I cleared out my savings...."

"No. Look I gotta' tell you..."

"I didn't go overboard, I took five thousand and bought lottery tickets ..."

"Holy crap!" (Actually, he said something more profane, but you get the point.)

"I know it doesn't sound like something I would do, but I did … and … I won!"

"You what?"

"I won a hundred thousand dollars. What I want your advice on is this."

"Shoot." (He is still using profanity.)

"So, do I pay the taxes out of the winnings, or buy more tickets to win bigger?"

I can't repeat what he said before the phone went dead. Thanksgiving is a long way off. I got a "For Sale" sign to put in the front yard when they come, and I'm picking up used lottery tickets everyday. I'm keeping them in a big glass bowl on the dining table. My brother will believe that I'm penniless.

My quest continues to even the score.

I told my friend, Peg, and she had a good idea. She thought I should make up cards and pass them around. I'd announce that the card they chose will indicate which pie they get, but all the cards read, "No Pie this Year."

Renewal

Hugo Stewart, 50-ish, balding, with tortoise-rimmed glasses perched on the end of his nose, sat at the kitchen table. "Our anniversary is coming up. Anything special you'd like to do?" he asked.

Jane Stewart, 40-ish, wearing denim capris with gardening gloves snapped to her belt served breakfast. The window near the table overlooked the gardens. Jane heard his question and looked out the window at the fruits of her efforts. The past three weeks she had gone down on her knees and weeded the beds, coaxed the blooms from their stalks, fertilized, and pruned. It was the perfect garden she had always wanted. She wondered if he noticed it.

"Let me think," she said.

"Okay," he said. He was reading the news headlines on his tablet, tapping into a story that was of interest, shaking his head and tapping somewhere else. Most of their conversations were conducted without eye contact. Did he care about celebrating their anniversary? Did she?

She pushed back her chair and carried the breakfast dishes to the sink. Was this the eighth or the ninth year? If it was an odd year, then their marriage contract was up for renewal. Other than the gardens, what else did she want to keep?

"Do you want another cup of coffee?" she asked.

"Sure," he muttered without checking his cup or looking away from the headlines.

She poured his coffee, then washed out the pot.

Later as she worked in the garden, her thoughts turned back to him. Had their relationship always been like this? Surely not, but truth be told, she wasn't sure anymore. Was he boring or was it her? Did she spend too much time in the garden and not enough... not enough what? she questioned. Shaking her head, she realized she might be ready for a change.

She called the ministry office and asked for a counseling appointment. It had been nine years since they had obtained their marriage license, and several years before that when she had not renewed her previous one. Laws and processes changed, she needed to come current on the hows, whats, and whens. Unlike the way it was long before, it was simple now. There were no courts, no alimony, no lawyers.

One party advised the ministry that they would not be renewing their license and the "available" sign went into the yard. The wife stayed in the home, and the husband left. "Available" meant more than just the home, it also meant the housewife. But she was the one who held all the cards as far as taking on another spouse, even on a temporary trial basis. Once you married, you were bound together for a minimum of three years, thereafter the license was up for renewal every odd year.

After the virtual counseling session, she logged into the ministry account and downloaded the form for non-renewal. She knew Hugo would not want to relocate from the area, so she copied the link for the current "availables" nearby, and scheduled it to be sent to him later. She would attach the customary "thanks for the memories" card. She scheduled the mail to arrive just before 5:00 p.m., insuring that he would receive it before leaving the office and thus avoiding a confrontation. She wondered if she would catch him by surprise or if this had been on his mind when he had asked her what she wanted for their anniversary.

Becoming available again, meant she was obligated to wear red. Men wore yellow, and she wondered if her husband still had the yellow tie and yellow sweater he had been wearing when they had first met. It was at a coffee house, the Bean-N-Leaf; he had come to be seen, she had come for the music. Friends of hers were playing in the band that night and the only open seat near the stage was at the table where he sat.

"Mind if I sit here?" she asked.

He looked at her, noticed the red scarf around her neck, and grinned.

"Friend of the band," she said nodding toward the stage.

"Yes," he said.

Yes to what she wondered. Yes to me sitting there, yes to the fact that I said I was friends with the band, yes to the possibility of hooking up with me?

What did it matter now? They had listened to the music, danced, and laughed on the crowded dance floor. There was interest on both their parts. They came back to that coffee house separately and were delighted to find each other there again. When was the last time they had been there? When was the last time they danced?

After lunch, she went to her closet and looked for the box marked "red." She had packed up all her "available" attire after they took their vows. Such a funny law. Until you are issued a marriage license, single women must wear red, single men must wear yellow. In each case, it must be prominently displayed in an outer garment such as a scarf, hat, or sweater. If any such attire is worn inappropriately, the wearer would be fined and lose all privileges. For a woman that meant she would lose her property; for a man, he would be banned from being married or available, for life. The only way around that was to choose banishment, which meant you hired onto a long distance ship and labored one way; never to return. She shuddered at the thought. Her second husband had met such a fate, having ventured into extra-marital affairs.

While in school, she studied the history surrounding these laws. What had gone before seemed beastly; sometimes the woman, and even a woman with children, had been turned out of the family home penniless while the man began a whole new family life without retribution. This was a better way, even if the costuming seemed silly.

She went to his closet and looked for his yellow sweater and tie. They were nowhere to be found. At the back of his closet, Jane found the deep purple shirt Hugo had worn that first time they had met; dancing in each other's arms. She wondered if he kept it for the memory.

She felt euphoric remembering the days of their falling in love. She took the shirt in her arms, eyes closed, danced in a circle, humming a tune. She longed for that feeling again.

Jane laid the shirt on the bed. She straightened it out, smoothing away the wrinkles.

Still humming, she went back to the computer and retrieved the email scheduled to be sent at five o'clock. She typed in a new message.

"Wear the shirt on the bed and meet me at the Bean-N-Leaf at seven. Garden club should be over by then."

Southern Hospitality

When I was eleven, I had to spend the summer with my Aunt Jenny, who had never married but lived with her mother, Granny Bea. They lived in the wild, in the swampy land between New Orleans and Mississippi. Mississippi to me was just the M-I-S-S, I-S-S, I-P-P-I of the jump rope song.

I rode the bus alone, my forehead pressed against the window; I watched mile after mile of lush trees standing alone in sometimes dusty roads, no houses in sight, as the road coursed and crossed waterways. My mother had put me on the bus outside of Phoenix, Arizona and told me it would be all day and night, all day and a second night, and by morning I would be there. It had been two days already, and night was coming. I was filled with anxiety and fear. This was my first trip alone into the South, as my mother called it. I had met both my Aunt and my Granny, but they had always come to visit us or been at a family gathering

The bus driver announced that we would soon be stopping for dinner and that we had just shy of an hour. "Get in, get fed, get washed up and on the bus, or you will be left behind," he said. I feared that I would miss the bus, but so far I had been timely in my return to the bus after breaks. He also said that while no passengers were getting off, we were picking up new passengers, so be ready to make room. I had been sitting in a row all alone for the trip so far. I hadn't thought about having to share that space, but now it weighed on my mind.

At the diner, I chose a stool at the counter. There was an old man on my left. I ordered half a ham sandwich. The money my mother had put in my hand was disappearing. I had no idea what food cost, and was surprised to see that the forty dollars was dwindling. I thought it would last for the return trip home as well but now was convinced I would starve to death before this dreadful summer was over.

"Ham sandwich," the old man said smacking his lips together, "that's a fine choice."

"Yes," I said, not sure if that had been a question.

"Should've got some of that tater salad," he said, "sure was good. Good as they come."

"No thank you," I said, being polite.

The waitress came and took his plate away. He thanked her and asked about pie.

"All baked fresh today. We got peach, apple, raisin and pear," she said.

"Pear pie. It's been a long time since I had that. I'll have that for sure." Then he leaned forward and whispered something to the waitress. I looked down at my empty plate and wondered what they talked about.

"Here you go," she said. She placed a slice of pear pie before me and another before the man.

"Um," I started to object and push it back.

"Compliments of the diner," she said. "We want to show you some southern hospitality, hon." She smiled at me and winked at the old man.

"Yum, pear pie," he said, as he forked a piece into his mouth. "Just like my momma used to make."

It sure looked good to me, and that ham sandwich hadn't been enough to fill me up or to quiet my nerves. I looked over at him; he nodded for me to eat the pie. So I pulled the plate to me and took a bite. It was what my Aunt Jenny would have called "plum delicious." That's what she said about all baked goods. She had the thick waist and plump cheeks to let you know that she didn't leave any sugary item sit too long. The pie crust was flaky and light, the way my mother baked them. I finished mine before the old man did.

"You like?" He asked.

"Yes, sir. It was real good." I smiled at him.

"Where you headed?" he asked.

"I'm on my way to my Granny's house in Brookhaven, halfway between New Orleans and Jackson, Mississippi."

"I know that town," he said. "I used to cross through it when I was going to Mobile. That's in Alabama."

I nodded. I had a map in my backpack. I looked at it often to be sure I was on the right bus going the right way, and to track how far I was from home, and how close I was getting to my destination.

"I have to spend the summer with my Granny and Aunt 'cuz my mother is running a campaign," I said to him, wondering if I was giving away too much information.

"Whose campaign?" he asked.

"Vance Hansen, Green Party candidate for senator in Arizona," I said.

He nodded. "Campaigning is mighty hard work. That's a good thing your mother is doing, and I'm glad you will have some time with your relatives, and get to know the south. Your Granny, is she a good cook?"

"I think so. My momma is," I said.

"Well you take some cooking lessons from her, now hear? You'll be thankful you did. My wife, now that woman can cook up a storm." He smiled.

"All aboard," the bus driver called from the doorway.

I had lost track of time. I got up, thanked the man, and took my bill to the register.

The waitress looked at it and smiled. "You're sure a lucky girl, the President paid for your sandwich and for the pie, too," she said.

"The President?" I asked.

"That was President Carter you were sitting and talking with girl, the most popular President ever!"

Back on the bus, I pulled out my diary and started on my essay for the first day of school when surely my teacher would ask me to write about the most important thing that had happened over the summer.

Angry Words

When I was nine, my mother took me to live with my Aunt Catherine. She was married to Uncle Peter, a war hero. They had two children, one a year older than me, the other a year younger. Shortly after I arrived, Peter came home missing a leg and nearly dead. They moved him into the bedroom and everyone stood around in hushed embarrassment. We didn't know what to say or do around him. He wasn't who he had been, the tall, athletic Peter Burrows; he was just the man in the bed with one leg.

But not to my Aunt Catherine. She said she was "hell bent on bringing him back." She brought in construction crews, and they transformed that wing of the house by adding a study and a parlor beside the huge bedroom and bathroom. In this way, she put him back into the center of things. If he were sleeping, we would sit in the study and read books and discuss things, or lie about in the parlor and practice our lines for the upcoming children's theater production of "Peter Pan." Catherine loved the theater and she encouraged us to "take to the stage."

There were many days when Peter didn't say a thing, then one day he seemed to wake up. He called to us to sit on the bed and talk with him. He asked us to practice our music, and the piano was moved into the parlor off his bedroom so he could listen.

"Bravo," he would shout and clap his hands when we finished. He didn't point out the odd sharp or flat, only encouragement.

"Another session this afternoon should do the trick," he once said to me, and he was right. The next time was much better.

As he healed, he sometimes sat in a chair or hobbled about on crutches. He was returning to the person he had been. No one was happier than Catherine. About this time, though, something changed between them. They were happy and spirited, but a black mood would overtake one or the other, and they would shout out angry words. As if on cue, we children would exit that wing of the house and find other things to do. I feared that they would divorce, and in that case wondered what would happen to me. My mother had not come back for me; I was happy to be with them, except for the angry words.

The anger though seemed short-lived. The doors would re-open, and we would gather again for music or conversation, or there were smiles all around in the dining room.

My mother returned the year I turned twelve and took me off to boarding school while she continued her travels. Catherine, Peter, and the children wrote to me, sent me packages of my favorite things and invited me back for the summer. During the year I had been away at school, Catherine had given birth to another daughter, and she was pregnant again.

When I asked my cousin, Gwenie who was fourteen, about her parents' angry rows, she stared at me.

"What? You thought they were really angry?"

"You heard them. They were mad."

"My mother told me they were only acting; she said sometimes they wanted to be alone. "

"What are you saying? They weren't really angry?"

"My mother is quite a good actress you know."

"I do, but..."

"My father was getting better; it meant that they could do things they hadn't been able to do."

"Like what?"

"Oh don't be such a baby! You know adult things...."

"Like?"

"Isn't it obvious? A new baby sister and another one on the way?"

"You mean?"

She leaned in close and whispered, "Sex."

An Ironic Life

Franklin Roosevelt Walker rose on the second ring of his alarm. He showered, shaved and dressed. Then took a bottle from under the Stetson hat on the top shelf of his closet, and tipped the fifth of vodka to his lips. He sighed heavily, replaced the bottle under the hat, and brushed his teeth.

In the kitchen, his wife, Nadine, handed him a mug of coffee. "Tonight be home at six," she said. "I'll have dinner on the table. We have a meeting at seven. This is important."

He nodded, gulped his coffee and bent down to kiss her on the cheek. He towered over her at six feet six inches. Nadine was a slight woman, barely five feet tall. He thanked God everyday for Nadine. He had nearly lost her eight years before. She, along with her three best friends had gone to dinner and on the return home, their car had been hit, head on. The driver and the front seat passenger were dead on impact. Nadine and the other passenger in the backseat were hospitalized for months. Nadine still had problems with balance and no longer drove. Thus her need for Franklin to accompany her to the meeting.

Franklin backed his car out of the garage and drove down the street; he pulled into the big church parking lot. He drove around to the back of the lot and retrieved the bottle from beneath his seat. He took a long swallow, recapped the bottle and replaced it, noting he would need to replace the bottle before the end of the day.

He was long past denial about being an alcoholic. He rationalized that he chose how he felt, and he felt better with a buzz. It gave him confidence; quieted the internal self-talk. In truth, he didn't feel he should have any of the life he had. None of it, not Nadine, not his job, not even his car. It was a collector's classic, a '63 Jaguar XKE and Joe, his mechanic, kept it in prime condition.

Franklin pulled out of the parking lot, weaving his way through Silicon Valley traffic to his office in a technology business park. He parked in the corner spot, a reserved space. From there, he could look out his office window at the car, a reminder of what he had, and what he kept under the seat.

The receptionist at the front desk, the accounting clerks and administrative staff looked up and acknowledged him as he passed down the hall to his office.

"Good Morning, Mr. Walker."

"Stock prices up today, sir."

"Good morning."

He nodded at each and picked up his mail from his secretary, positioned outside his corner office.

"Morning boss," Gloria said. She would summarize the stack of pink phone message slips she passed to him. "Steve in NE sales office needs a call back about a client before nine. Advertising agency here for presentation at eleven. Bob in Accounting needs your signature, and I have our French distributor on hold regarding the last shipment."

He took the stack of papers, nodded to Gloria and plopped down in the leather chair behind his mahogany desk. He picked up the receiver and said "Philippe, what's the story..."

That was how this day and every day started. By 10:30 a.m., he had put out the fires and everything was back on an even keel. It took a lot out of him. He wondered how he became CEO of this company and how long before someone saw through him and fired him. On the other hand, everyone seemed incompetent, none of them could cross a "t" or dot an "i" without him. He called Gloria via the intercom.

"Gloria, I've got a few more call to make. I don't want to be disturbed."

"You got it, boss," she said.

He rose and closed the door. He punched the do not disturb button on his phone, then opened the bottom desk drawer where tucked behind the hanging file folders was a quart of Stoli vodka. Better if it came from the freezer, but this would have to do. He gulped down what he considered two fingers, just enough to keep the glow of vitality. He snickered at the thought.

At 11:00 a.m., he walked down the hall to the conference room. He wondered if the advertising agency would propose some viable ideas today, if not it was time to fire them. With what they paid Tattersby and Connor in a monthly retainer, they should be getting high-quality ads and a campaign to rattle the bones of their competitors. He straightened up, throwing back his shoulders, pushed out his chest. He was solidly in control as he entered the conference room.

Marion Wallace, the director of marketing, introduced the PR and advertising personnel to Mr. Walker, and Peter Jacobson, the VP of Marketing. She laid out the technical aspects of the new product and its target market and key dates to satisfy the sales department. She then turned over the meeting to the agency personnel to present their comprehensive campaign.

The senior account exec from Tattersby and Connor had barely gotten through the first few slides when Franklin slapped the palm of his right hand on the table and said, "Wait a second. I'm a bit confused. If we are such a contender in this market and an important client, why aren't Mr. Tattersby and Ms. Connor here?"

The account exec tried to relate that he and his team were the actual people working on the plan. Marian nudged Peter Jacobson, who tried to assure Franklin the intent of the meeting today was to hear the agency's PR and advertising plans and select the ads for print.

"This is a working meeting," Peter Jacobson said.

"Then why am I here? Why do you need the CEO in this meeting?"

No one said anything. They looked from one to another, then dropped their gaze to their hands, fiddling with the papers in front of them.

Franklin huffed and stood. "There is no reason for this meeting. A waste of my time." He marched out. As he left, he heard Marion apologize, and Peter say they should reconvene at the agency's office as soon as possible, or deadlines would be missed.

Franklin stopped by the CFO's office and asked if he was open to go to lunch. Roger Fitzpatrick nodded and swept the papers from his desk into the top drawer and locked it. As they walked out of the building, Franklin said, "You drive Roger."

"Sure," Roger said. "Where to?"

"The Bistro."

Roger smiled. Franklin always chose The Bistro. It was an old-fashioned steakhouse with a full bar, dim-lit booths and never very busy. Experience told him it would be a double vodka shot lunch with maybe a French dip sandwich. Roger wasn't going to complain. He knew Franklin came to him when he needed to vent. Roger got this job because he and Franklin had worked together long ago. Franklin had been a project manager and Roger the cost accountant. He had listened when Franklin needed someone, and he kept his mouth shut the rest of the time. He did what Franklin told him to do, and documented it well.

Franklin ranted about Peter and his staff, about the inept advertising agency, and about their lack of protocol. He felt snubbed to be included in a meeting where his peers were not present.

"It was all about how he looked and nothing about getting the job done," Marian complained to Peter as they drove across town from the advertising agency office.

"Well, I think we kept the peace, but..." Peter said.

"I know what you are going to say," said Marion. "What top notch agency wants to go balls out for us when we have that egotistical bastard at the helm."

Peter started to say something, but Marian's cell phone rang.

"Sheesh," she said recognizing the caller id.

"Who is it?" Peter asked.

"Trent." Trent was her engineering counterpart. The call could go either way. Trent was a terrific engineer and Marian enjoyed working with him, but he was also an old crony of Franklin's which meant sometimes he got swayed, and circumvented the agreed upon specifications. Marion answered the call and put it on speaker.

"Trent."

"What the hell's going on?"

"I don't know. What did you hear?" Marian shrugged her shoulders at Peter.

"Franklin called and read me the riot act. Said there's no reason for me to be working engineering on this product without marketing. Said marketing has their heads up their ass. That's a direct quote. You know it's not my opinion."

"Shit! We had a presentation today for PR and advertising for the product roll out. You know how Franklin won't let us move forward without him on every detail..."

"Yeah, I know."

"Well, the agency gets through two slides. Two slides, Trent, and Franklin goes ballistic about why he's in the meeting but the agency principles aren't. He calls it a waste of time and storms out."

"Shit!" Trent said. "Sorry..."

Marian sighed. "Yep me too. Peter and I went over to the agency, worked through the presentation, fine toothed the plan, selected the ads... We're ready for the roll out, but we need Franklin's okay. Today's not that day."

"Maybe tomorrow."

"Right."

"We'll talk, in the morning."

"Call me on my cell phone."

"Keep the faith. We've had to work through issues like this before."

"Thanks."

Marian and Peter looked at each other.

"Not much more we can muck up today," they said in unison and laughed.

Franklin returned from lunch around 1:30 p.m. He didn't go back to his office, he sat in Roger's office and discussed the 49'ers chances for the super bowl.

Several manufacturing managers came to check on inventory approvals needed by the CFO and were drawn into the conversation. It was easy to forget his worries when he was in this state of mind, happy, carefree, content to be talking football. In his youth, he had been a formidable quarterback and talking football took him back to when he knew he was good at something. Not like now.

At three, the talk had circled several times and was running out of steam. Franklin rose, slapped his knees and said he had a couple of errands to run for his wife. He ambled through the office to his car.

Peter Jacobson and Marian watched Franklin drive away.

"One day we should follow him," Marian said.

"I know. Every day at three, he's got errands to run for his wife. And..."

"When he comes back, nothing gets done." Marian finished.

"There aren't many minutes when he's really sober," Peter said.

Franklin drove directly to JJ's Liquor Store. He set two quarts and three fifths of Stoli on the counter.

"Party?" the pert young clerk asked.

"You could say that," Franklin said. "Gifts for my friends actually." He replayed what he had said fearing he had slurred "actually."

"You're a generous man."

"Thank you."

Franklin placed the bottles in the trunk of the car, wrapping each in the folds of a blanket. He replaced the almost empty under the front seat after draining the last swallow from that bottle. "Good night friend," he said and dropped it out the window along the side of the road before he returned to the office.

He sat at his desk, door closed, phone off the hook, eyes shut until 5:30 p.m. This had become his daily ritual, drink enough to put the lights out, lay low. Every day he hated himself for drinking. He hated who and what he had become. He had tried, really tried to taper off. It was hopeless. Quietly he opened his drawer, popped a mint in his mouth, and drove home.

As Nadine had said, dinner was on the table at six and at seven, they were present at the Mothers Against Drunk Drivers meeting. Nadine had a productive day. She had managed twenty phone calls to public officials, judges and prosecutors lobbying for stronger sentences, larger fines, and stricter penalties for drunk drivers. MADD was Nadine's passion, her mission in life since the accident. The driver who hit them was drunk, and it was his fifth arrest for driving under the influence.

Later, Franklin helped Nadine from her bath, and only when she was asleep, did he retrieve the bottles from the car. He replaced the empties and finished off the bottle under the Stetson hat.

Each day was similar to the previous; Franklin tried to maintain a balance between sobriety and inebriation and attended MADD meetings with his wife. After a sales dinner with prospective clients one night, Franklin headed home. He stumbled to the car, fumbled with the keys, and pulled out onto the highway.

Not far from home, he noticed flashing lights in the rearview mirror. Their presence was enough to sober him up. He maneuvered the car through the lanes of traffic and was about to pull off to the right when he calculated the consequences. There was little chance to avoid a DUI; then Nadine would know the truth, and he would lose her. A DUI also would put him at risk of losing his job, his bonuses, and reputation. All this might leave him bankrupt, financially and socially. He weighed the alternatives.

He checked again for the lights in the mirror, then stomped on the accelerator and took the exit toward the reservoir. He sped up, although the road narrowed and wound through the hills. At the hairpin turn with a view of the reservoir below, he gunned the engine and barreled through the barrier. The car sailed through the air, tumbled down the embankment, and plunged nose first into the reservoir. Franklin's hands gripped the steering wheel. The windows were open, and he braced for the icy water. His cell phone pinged indicating he had voicemail.

The ambulance turned off the freeway past the reservoir and attended to an emergency call. Nadine Walker had fallen and broken her hip.

The Invitation

Betty looked into the mirror and readjusted the curly auburn wig on her head. She bought the wig for the way it enhanced her green eyes. She had chosen an emerald green dress and her black wool coat thinking the overall look was classy, sophisticated and hid well her real age. Betty never liked to think of herself at her real age; she liked to think of herself at her "mental age." Even as she thought this, her hands flew up and put quotation marks in the air. She smiled at her reflection feeling satisfied with herself. "I'm going to pull it off," she said aloud to no one.

She picked up the invitation left on the entry table. She ran her hand over the embossed letters. "This is real classy," she thought. "Not those ink jet printed things. This is a real classy invitation. This is the way our wedding invitations will be."

Betty thought that she could cheat old age with a little makeup and a wig, but Betty no longer had a firm grip on reality.

Betty had a crush on Burt ever since the summer Betty was fourteen. Burt worked as the lifeguard at the neighborhood pool, and Betty had gone to the pool every day that Burt was there. She secretly dreamed of their future together and had concocted a story every day. None of these stories had ever played out, but Betty had clung to the idea that she and Burt were meant for each other even through the passage of sixty years.

The invitation in her hand was to the wedding of Burt's grandson, Marcus. Betty had tried to be a part of the circle of Burt's friends, and while she may have been in the same room, she had never received so much as a nod of acknowledgment or recognition from Burt. The invitation in her hand had not been addressed to her. While attending a wake for a friend, she had seen it on the desk and stole it. Betty had stooped to being a thief, anything to be a part of Burt's life. Now that his wife had died, he was unburdened and free. Betty had every intention of making sure that she and Burt would finally be together.

She placed the invitation in her purse and took another look in the mirror. "Our eyes will meet across the room..." she began the daydream. "He'll come to me, take my hand and say that he has been searching for me all these years."

"Good gracious Miss Betty! What are you up to?" The attendant looked at Betty who stood in front of the mirror at the entrance to the retirement home. "You haven't got a stitch of clothes on. Let's get you back to your room."

What's Wrong with Online Dating

On paper he was perfect! Perfect for me! He was on the Internet; the singles match up site. I read his profile a dozen times and sat looking at his photos several nights in a row before I pressed the "contact" key. I had been sitting on my high hopes for several months telling myself, this time, HE (the proverbial perfect match) would find me, but I jumped the gun.

The last guy I met online had seemed perfect too, but we got off on the wrong foot. In truth, I lost interest when over a cup of coffee, he told me that he and his wife split when he retired, and she did not. He had devised a plan to move out of the city, but because she wouldn't quit her job, they divorced. As I was still working, I didn't see that there was much future for us.

Joe in Seattle responds that he has been looking at my profile too, and happy to have me contact him. He has been single again for seven years. Would I like to meet for a glass of wine on Thursday at seven?

There is a lot here to discern. He is telling me that he was once married or in a relationship, but he could also be in a relationship now. Why would he suggest Thursday? Is he telling me that he is already busy, or not going to tie up a weekend night with me? He drinks and expects me to drink too. Is he an alcoholic or a recovering one looking to ward off any bad relationships? No, they always start by telling you that they don't drink alcohol. I go back and read his profile which I have bookmarked. No, his profile doesn't say any of that. I need to check if Thursday will even work for me. If I say "yes," then am I copping to how lonely I am, that I am too eager, or don't have a social life? If I say "no," am I saying that I don't meet guys in bars, or that I am too busy to start a relationship?

This is what is wrong with online dating. You start off with high hopes, and you end up a bundle of nerves questioning every word, syntax, and punctuation. "Should I have used the exclamation mark or will he think I am a snob using a semicolon in a text message?" I haven't begun to fret about what to wear.

I once matched up with a professional psychologist. He let it be known during our online interaction that he was all about the full-breasted figure. I wore a loose fitting shirt over a low-cut camisole. I wasn't taking the shirt off until he showed some interest in me before he could take a look at mine. I became dismayed when he took the check from the waitress and told me what my portion was. He walked me back to my car and asked me a personal question that was beyond my scope of first date questions. "What's your gas mileage?" I smiled, took my shirt off, and drove away.

Back to Thursday. I have most of the afternoon free. Plenty of time to get a manicure, pedicure, try on four to six outfits to find the right one, and be on time for the date. Wait! It's not a date, and I haven't even responded. Now he will wonder why I have taken so long to respond. He will wonder if I am who I said I am. If the photos are really of me or of someone, I may have met. I dated a guy who told me he met a woman online who kept putting him off about meeting in public. She was young, gorgeous and in great shape from the photos. He was attracted to her and wanted to have a face-to-face conversation. Finally, she fessed up, she was a bit older than she had led him to believe, and she was a couple of hundred pounds over weight, but working on taking it off. She needed someone in her life to keep her at it. The photos were of her daughter at high school graduation; she had once looked just like that.

So it is important to meet to ensure that you are conversing with who you think they are. So I should say, "yes" to a meeting. If not, he will assume that if I am unwilling to meet in public, that I am either not available, or not interested in anything but an online relationship. He will wonder if I have eight children or fifty cats? Unless he has eight children and needs a mother for them. Did I say anything in my profile that would make him think that I would be a perfect mother for his eight children? OMG!

That's another reason why online dating doesn't go anywhere. Pretty soon the guy who looked so perfect has morphed into the worst imaginable nightmare date. The guy who won't take "no," and follows you home, sits on the curb across the street, sighing into the night because he is so in love with you.

No, that would be the guy who cries over dinner about his last girlfriend who moved away to get away from him. He didn't understand why she did that. She wouldn't even meet with him to explain. Then he looks into your eyes and tells you that you look exactly like her. (Wait, it gets worse.) Two days later you pick up the newspaper, and there is his picture. He tracked down the ex-girlfriend, (and yes, you do look a lot like her) and he murdered her as she slept. She only lived two blocks away from you. Then he shot and killed himself. (Talk about dodging a bullet!)

Back to Thursday. He didn't say where to meet, so I take the initiative and pick a place I know. I want a wine bar or bistro, not a bar with flashing beer signs in the window and a pool table. I want to pick a place where we can have an hour of quiet conversation to see if there is any chemistry. (Oh, not that word. I hate that when guys write in their profile that they are looking for chemistry. Is it a code word for sex? What if women were very explicit about what physical contact they wanted. Often when meeting online, a man will let you know that he expects it to become a physical relationship. He is not going to put up with this online conversing too long before there is some action. I have fantasized responding: "Sex on our first meeting? No problem but isn't that too much pressure to perform? Because it could ruin your chance for a second date."

Ah Chemistry! Is it a fragrance? Note to self – create an alluring metrosexual perfume and sell it as "Chemistry." I can see the smoky chanteuse in the low-cut clinging gown with the Lauren Bacall voice whispering, "Chemistry, there is no mystery when you wear Chemistry." Or "Chemistry, the catalyst behind every great love affair."

Back to Thursday. I look at the clock, three hours have passed since he messaged about meeting. I message back. "How about Wine on the Waterfront. I'll be the one with a glass of red." Cute, pert, a little sassy but it certainly doesn't contain any of my neurotic ramblings.

That was Tuesday, and now it's nearly midnight on Wednesday, and I haven't heard back from him. Did I take too long? Does he not like red wine drinkers? Does he not like his ladies to pick the place? Is he Google-ing to try and find if "Wine on the Waterfront " is a bar? Does he not want to meet in a wine bar because he doesn't like wine, but he is a beer guy? Oh, so he doesn't have the six-pack abs like in the photo, but a nice round beer gut because he hangs out drinking beer every night? No wonder he didn't respond, he fell asleep with his face in a bowl of stale pretzels? Or in bed with the barmaid, you know, the one with a single tooth? Or he doesn't keep track of his messages, and he was messaging with more than me, so when I finally responded, he thought the reply came from Twyla in Tukwila or Polly in Puyallup?

I Google-ed "Wine on the Waterfront." How many are there? I was thinking of the one here in Green Lake. Is it too high class? Maybe he doesn't drive? Maybe he doesn't have a car? Maybe he has never worked a day in his life and is a serial gigolo in-between gigs. What did I say in my profile that would have attracted him?

Oh yeah, I contacted him.

A Patient Man

Wednesday

I limped home after working a full shift at the senior center. My back was killing me, my left foot dragging. I popped bread into the toaster and opened the last can of sardines. I ate all but one and gave that to the cat, Mr. McGreggor. Funny name for a cat, but that was what Bobby named her all those years ago, and I never thought to change it. Mr. McGreggor was actually the third in a line of felines all bearing the same name. When she finished licking out the sardine can, she mewed at my chair. I picked her up and nestled her.

"Not too bad for an old cat," I said to her as I scratched behind her ears, and at the base of her tail. She purred roughly. We both nodded off.

Thursday

I woke late, the sun already over the horizon. I jerked myself over to hang my legs off the bed. I couldn't straighten up. I was bent over at a forty-five-degree angle and listing to the left. I peed myself at the toilet, then cursed old age. I dropped a towel to the floor to mop up, using my foot to move the towel around and decided to shower. I huddled under the stream of hot water until it was only warm, but couldn't get any movement from my hunched over posture. I could hear Mr. McGreggor mewing to be let out.

"Hold on Mister, I've got to get things working here," I said.

She mewed her need back.

When the water was cold, I shut it off and stood shivering. I still couldn't stand upright. I was already late for the center, so decided to skip it. I reached for the towel and dried myself. I grabbed the shower curtain as usual, but the rod came crashing down, and I slipped and fell on my butt. My head ratcheted back and hit the wall. I saw stars.

The stars hung there in front of me, and I thought about romantic nights when Mary and I used to sit under the stars out on Overlook Road. I knew she had died four years ago from the cancer, but still, I remember thinking I should call and see if she would like to go out with me, and look at the stars again. Funny how time got mixed up, unless time is all mixed up, and we are the ones who try and string it out in some order.

Some time later Mr. McGreggor was licking my face. The old girl must've thought I had died.

"I'm okay girl, just got mixed up for a while. Let's get moving now."

I twisted around and got up on my knees and with my hands on the side of the tub, I pushed myself back into a standing position and climbed out. I put on my bathrobe and found that I could come to a fully upright posture.

"By gawd, that fall straightened me out."

I let Mr. McGreggor out the back door and poured myself a glass of orange juice, took a can of Fancy Feast off the shelf and opened it. I knew I should call in, and let them know I wasn't going to be able to volunteer today, but I never got around to it.

Friday

I liked to go fishing on Fridays. I set my sights on a trout like the one I caught years ago when Bobby was a boy. I remembered that a nice bit of sand crab was what caught that fish, and I hooked one on the end of the line. I stood midstream in my waders with the flow pushing against me, and I cast my line into the shallows at the curve where the water was still. Fishing is a patient man's sport. I have always been a patient man. After some time I realized I was shivering.

"C'mon fish. It's time for both of us to get warmed up. You in a frying pan, me in front of the fireplace."

I felt a tug and then a pull, and I knew I had him. I played out the line and reeled him in. He was a big one, maybe four pounds.

"Looky here Bobby; we got us our lunch."

Bobby grinned from ear to ear. "Let me hold him."

The photo showed Bobby holding up the fish. He remembered that trip different from me. It's funny how memory does that. I thought we walked down to the river and dropped our lines; he remembered it as a weeklong camping trip. Either way, it was a long time ago.

Out of my waders, I shivered lying on the bed. I couldn't get warm. It was a bone-aching cold, and the bed wasn't as soft as it used to be.

Saturday

I got married on a Saturday when I was twenty-two. Mary was to arrive at the church at a quarter to eleven, and I was supposed to be there waiting. I got a flat tire out on Highway 99 and had to change it myself. I stripped out of my jacket and dress shirt. I changed that flat as quickly as I could but arrived at the church late, after eleven.

"Where in tarnation you been boy?" Mary's father yelled.

"Got a flat tire, Mr. Pierson."

"Where's your shirt and tie?"

"In the back seat. I took them off to keep them clean."

His face was red as he yelled at me and I understood how he was trying to protect his little girl. I looked toward the church and saw Mary. She was so beautiful. She didn't want me to see her in that dress until she walked down the aisle, but I was looking at her then.

Thinking about Mary brought tears to my eyes. We were married fifty-three years last June. I lost her before our fiftieth anniversary. She had tried to make it to that day, but her body quit on her. I miss her.

Sunday

I heard bells and thought it must be Sunday. I rarely missed a service, but I couldn't get a move on. I thought about that for a minute. I remembered falling in the tub, and suddenly I was back in the tub, only the pain was in my head, not my back. Did that mean I had been here in the tub for three days? Has that much time passed or only an hour? When my mind wanders, I lose track of time.

I remember the day Mary and I sat on the sofa watching Bobby outside riding his bicycle. We were all smiles and holding hands because today was the day that the court filed our permanent adoption papers. For five years we loved him as our own, but the Services could take him away. Now he was ours.

Suddenly, it's Bobby's graduation, and we were the proudest parents. Neither Mary nor me went beyond high school, and now we had a college graduate. Bobby stood tall and shook the hand of the college president, who held his diploma. Later I unrolled it and saw that it was only a blank piece of paper.

"They just use that for the ceremony," Bobby said.

I think of all the money we paid for him to receive this blank piece of paper.

Mr. McGreggor mewed, but I couldn't see her. I worried about her safety. Oddly I'm not thinking about mine. I'm either in a state of shock or already dead, I reason.

There was a time I was in my uniform, home on leave, seriously contemplating going AWOL. What that Army recruiter didn't tell me was that the opportunity they were giving me was to come back maybe alive. I had a wife, and I didn't want to make her a widow. I couldn't stand the thought of us not having all those years ahead. We could have children, make a home, grow old together. I wanted that more than anything. The chaos of fighting the war was inhumane. I had enlisted gung-ho and full of patriotism, now I was pessimistic.

I had buddies who died, some were maimed, and one went crazy and shot himself in the foot rather than go back into combat. Mary convinced me to go back and finish my duty.

"I'll be here waiting for you," she said.

I heard church bells again and wondered if it was just the phone. I'm fading in and out, switching between this time and other times.

Back to the church and the wedding, only this was Bobby's wedding. Mary and I watch his bride in a cloud of white take her place beside him. Later, when we danced, Mary said this was better than our wedding because she was enjoying herself today.

"What do you mean? You didn't enjoy yourself at our wedding?"

"Not like this. I was a bundle of nerves. I remember when you weren't there at the church, all I could think was that you changed your mind."

"Changed my mind? I was afraid you would come to your senses and not want to marry me."

And we laughed at our youth and our insecurities.

At some point, I heard knocking on the front door. For me to hear it all the way back here, they had to be pounding. I wondered who it was. The door was probably unlocked because I wasn't good about locking up every night. I hoped they would come in.

I wondered if Mary was still waiting for me.

In the Air

Papa owned a circus. It was back in the old country and not anything like the circuses today. I grew up under the big tent, in and around all the people and animals. I was no stranger to the high flyers, the clowns, the elephant trainers and the lion tamer.

Over the years, distance had grown between us. Father had seemed steeped in the old ways while I was young, and embraced our new country, our new culture, my new life. My father died at eighty-seven, and it left me shocked. Shocked and dismayed that I had not reconnected with him. I had not hated my father but loved him. As a young boy, I had idolized my father.

When he died, the lawyer read his will and the only thing he left me was a key.

"You always loved this key, keep it with you, and it will protect you," the lawyer read and handed me the key. The key was old-fashioned; a long shaft with a fancy brass head stamped with a third eye, and it was strung on a waxed linen cord. I took it and wondered if there was anything it opened. It felt familiar in my hand, and I bounced it in my palm, feeling its weight. The lawyer had no information on the key other than my father's words.

My father didn't leave much of an estate; the circus had disbanded long ago, no land holdings, a little furniture that went to my sister. She turned up her nose and said, "junk." My sister and I had been there for the reading of the will. My only connection to the family of late was my sister. We had lost touch with other family members.

I left the office and examined the key. I considered consulting a clairvoyant, or fortuneteller. Perhaps a meeting with a medium might reveal some hidden meaning or treasure. My father's sister had once held séances and readings. Where was Magdalena now?

I retraced my steps to the lawyer's office and asked for information on other family members. Certainly, he had to contact them regarding the closing of the estate. The lawyer handed me a list of typed names and addresses, many crossed out or notations written nearby. One name stood out as I looked over the list, Oscar Valenzuela. Who was this? Could this be the wrestler, Uncle Oscar, who had once been in the circus? From my boyhood, I remembered him for his daring feat of wrestling bears. His name was crossed out and "deceased" written next to it. Was he truly a relative? I scanned the names for Magdalena. She was there, listed as Maggie, which had a much less dramatic flair, but her address and phone number were nearby. It seemed my aunt lived in the next town, a short distance from me. I made plans to contact her and visit.

I became excited about the possibility of the key fitting, unlocking some treasure. It didn't have to be money, something personal about my father, or our family heritage.

As I crossed the street, I saw a faded red VW bug. The bumper sticker offered excellent advice, "The Best Things in Life Aren't Things." I smiled making the connection with my own thoughts. I wanted to reconnect with my family and find closure with my father.

Up the street, I saw an orange Corvette polished to a gloss finish. It didn't slow down for me in the crosswalk, but sped up and clipped me behind the knees. It lifted me, sent me flying in an arc over the cars and buildings, into the air. At that moment, I remembered being on the trapeze swing with my father, the greatest trapeze artist of his day. Felix Souza! He performed for kings and queens in all the capitals of Europe. I became aware of the downside of the arc, and in the path ahead was the concrete embankment of an overpass. My arms and legs flailed in the air. Around my neck hung the key. The sun glinted off its surface.

From the sky, two hands appeared, outstretched to me. I lifted my arms, offered my hands; the hands grasped mine, encircling my wrists. Our hands locked in a familiar way, fingers encircling wrists. I was lifted into another arc. Swinging upward, I could clearly see the safety of the trapeze platform.

Butch

On Friday, I had too much to drink, and so did he. Butch was my boyfriend. At forty-four, he's way too much boy and not much of a friend. I've known for some time there's no future for us, that I would never ride off into the sunset with him, but I procrastinated (and drank) and was still with him. I started surfing the web looking at other places I might want to live, thinking about how I could pack the car and disappear.

That night, we staggered out of the pub after he got into a fistfight over a stupid dart game. I was trying to catch up to him, to see which of us was in better shape to drive. I got halfway to the car and threw up. I was down on my knees puking into a handicap space. I watched him rev the engine and throw it into reverse. When he saw me retching, I heard him curse; then he took off. I looked up and watched the tail lights fade into the night.

"Really? You're leaving me here?"

Then I cursed him. That's when the plan took shape. I knew he would go over to our other hangout bar and get wasted. He might tell Big Bug to come and get me, but I couldn't count on it. I walked back into the bar and asked Rosa to drive me home.

"Are you kidding me? He left you in the lot puking your guts out?"

"Now," I said, calm and loud. "Let's go now."

"What's your big hurry?" she said sliding off the barstool. Her purse was in her hand, and she was fishing for the keys.

She pulled up to the apartment, and I checked for lights. His car was nowhere to be seen. Not like last week when he left it in the middle of the street idling and fell asleep on the couch. The apartment was dark. I thanked Rosa and made my way up the stairs. I tried the door, unlocked it and went straight to the bedroom. I pulled down my suitcase and emptied the drawers into it. I filled the laundry basket with the rest of my clothing. After emptying the trash bin into the tub, I loaded it with my cosmetics and curling irons, blow dryers, and every other girlie thing I had in the cupboard.

There was nothing of value in the kitchen, everything bought second hand and worn out or mismatched. I stood in the living room and looked at the big plasma television I bought him for the Super Bowl. I didn't have the time or strength to pull that down. I wondered if I tuned it to ESPN he might not notice I was gone for a couple of days. The spite in me was rising, thinking about him high tailing it out of the lot. I took the scissors and cut the plug off the end of the cord.

I lugged the baskets down to my car and into the hatch, ran back up and brought down the suitcase. I grabbed his gym bag and filled it with my shoes.

After one more look around, I decided nothing was worth losing my lead, and left.

It was after midnight when I pulled onto the interstate. He knew I had come from the South; he'd suspect I would go to my best friend's or my sister's, so I went in the opposite direction. I couldn't call either of them because they were best friends and horrible liars. It would take me three hours to cross the state line, and I wanted to be there before he got wise to me.

On the road, I drove with the windows down and sang along with the songs on the radio. I wondered how much alcohol was still in my system and knew I was coming down hard when I started feeling bad about leaving him. This wasn't the first time I had packed up and fled. Once before, I skedaddled, but I turned around and went back before he knew I was gone. I went to an AA meeting and started working on my self-esteem. I needed to do that again. I gave myself a good talking to about how I deserved a lot better, and I wasn't the one who left him in the parking lot.

At 3:12 a.m. I read the "Welcome to Wyoming" sign and headed north toward Montana. I stopped at the first motel, pulling my car around to the back of the lot. I got a room and asked for a wake-up call at 8:00 a.m. That would be enough resting time, keeping me ahead of him. As I lay on the too-hard bed staring up at the smoke detector light on the ceiling, I worried that maybe he wouldn't even care that I was gone. Did I want him to come looking for me? I replayed all those movies where the mistreated woman ran off, changed her hair, her name, and started over; then the man found her. Right, there was my second mistake. I twisted and turned, and suffered one nightmare after another. In one, Julia Roberts' husband in "Sleeping With The Enemy" morphed into Freddy Krueger. I awoke awash in sweat. The clock blinked 5:33 a.m. That was enough for me. I showered, put on fresh clothes and left the key in the room.

The highway was dark, no traffic. I was happy to see the golden arches ahead and pulled in for some coffee and a breakfast sandwich. The food tasted good. I ticked off the miles to Glacier National Park. The first sign read three hundred sixty-eight miles and by sunrise, it was two hundred fifty-three miles. I pushed to reach there by lunch; I bought a lot of fast food snacks when I gassed up. Fritos are my all time favorite, and I hadn't had any in years. I finished the first bag and started on the second in less than an hour. Now I had to worry about gaining fifty pounds before I was "far enough" away from Butch.

What kind of name was Butch anyway? That was the first mistake all those years ago. I should have kept on walking when I heard his name.

Three Words

She set breakfast on the table and sat down. She poked her fork into the scrambled eggs and veggies, brought it to her lips, blew gently, and smiled, satisfied with the taste.

"Rock Hat Shoe," he said.

She looked at her husband and tried to keep the growing contempt from her face, shrugged, knowing that he wasn't registering what was happening any way. She hated what her life had become.

"Rock Hat Shoe," he said again.

She gave him a tight-lipped grimace and nodded her head toward the eggs. He followed her gaze, looking into his plate.

"Rock Hat Shoe," he said, starting to cry.

She reached across the table, picked up his fork, bringing it first to her lips to be sure it was not too hot, then to his lips. His lips remained shut.

"Open," she commanded.

"Rock Hat Shoe," he said again.

"I don't know what that means," she said

"Rock Hat Shoe," he said with even more conviction.

Was he really trying to communicate with her, trying to tell her something or was this just a random assortment of sounds that his brain retrieved. Because he repeated it five times, she tried to make sense of it.

After breakfast, she led him out onto the porch, into his favorite chair. She asked him if he was chilly, then laid a plaid wool blanket over his lap and legs, and went back to clear the table. When she returned with the remains of her coffee, she found him asleep. She sighed, and went back to the kitchen.

At dinner, it was the same routine. She nodded toward the fork waiting with the bite of chicken and mashed potatoes. His favorite, she thought.

"Try it. It's smashed potatoes like you like."

He looked at her, his eyes not focusing. He looked past the food on the idling fork and off into the other room.

"Rock Hat Shoe," he said softly. He opened his mouth and took the food. He chewed slowly, methodically, and swallowed. He waited, lips poised for another bite. She loaded up the fork and lifted it to his lips. They fell into a rhythm; she would feed him a bite, feed herself and back to him until he indicated that he wanted no more, or the food was gone. Pushing back from the table, she took the dishes to the sink. She brought a cloth and washed his face.

"Movie?" she asked hoping that they could spend an hour cuddled on the lounge watching an old favorite. For that time, they'd be the couple they used to be.

"Rock Hat Shoe," he said. His words were simple but lacked meaning. She stood ready, waiting to see what he would do. He did nothing.

Later she helped him shed his clothes, wash, put on his pajamas and get into bed. She hesitated as she helped him settle, tucked in the blankets and kissed him softly.

"Oh," he said when their lips met. She pulled back and looked into his eyes. For a moment he was the handsome dark-haired conductor wearing his black tails with the baton in his hand, and she was the first violin, staring up into his twinkling eyes. For a moment, there was that old connection, the recognition, the wanting.

Then it was gone

She tiptoed out of the room, down the hall, into the den. She nestled into the armchair and opened her book. She never imagined their life would be like this. They had planned to travel, to explore; they were still young and vital. She was; he was not. How long would this last? How long could she keep him at home, care for him? At what cost? When he was gone would she be old and unable to fulfill those adventures? Would she be too spent to enjoy life?

Her frustration rose, she wanted to hurl the book across the room. She wanted to give in to the fury, pick up the stack of plates she had unloaded from the dishwasher and smash each one. Knowing the noise would alarm and frighten him, she quieted herself, stuffed the corner of the lap blanket into her mouth and sobbed.

Spent from the tears, she padded back to the bedroom, climbed into bed alongside her husband. He acknowledged her, spooning her. In the still of the night, she heard him whisper, "Rock Hat Shoe."

Doing The Right Thing

Laura sits at the dressing table looking into the mirror. She recognizes her mother's face in her own. She picks up the hairbrush; beginning at the scalp pulls the brush through her long hair. She counts each brush stroke, "One, two, three..." She remembers sitting at her mother's feet, her mother brushing Laura's hair. She counted out the hundred brush strokes as she taught her daughter the importance of proper hair grooming.

"You have such beautiful hair. It's a mix of my auburn hair and your father's blond hair. In the sunlight, your hair glows full of sun."

Laura brushes the hair on the right and then on the left; long strokes and counts each out "Eleven, twelve, thirteen..." Today marks the first anniversary of her husband, Peter's death. Laura rose as usual, but she has nowhere to go. No one is waiting for her; no one will be calling her. She bathed and did her once monthly moisturizing treatment on her hair; leaving it piled high on her head while she soaked in the tub; then rinsed it thoroughly before braiding it, and letting it dry in the sun.

The auburn color has faded over the years and is streaked through with gray. She thinks of the gray as the maturing of the golden highlights of her youth. She remembers when she first married Peter, he would sit and brush her hair as they watched television. He held a handful of her hair and commented on the weight of it. She pulls a section over her shoulder and brushes it, counting, "Twenty-two, twenty-three, twenty-four..." When the children were little, and they stuck their sticky fingers in her hair, she had thought about cutting it. "No," Peter said. Instead, she pulled it into a ponytail or braided it down her back.

Peter stares at her through the silver-framed photo on the dressing table. Her Peter. They were always happy together. She hadn't expected to live out this year without him. A year of missing him; a year of looking back.

She believes if she does the right things, if she maintains proper hair care, she will be rewarded. Her hair is clean, the ends trimmed. It has been all the way down her back and then cut back to shoulder length and grown out again and again. She pulls another section over her shoulder and continues brushing "Twenty-nine, thirty, thirty-one..."

When her sister, Barbara, underwent chemo treatments and lost her hair, Laura cut off enough for the wig maker. Laura watched her sister pull the wig on and laughed out loud when Barb began her impersonation of Laura. Tears well up, she brushes harder trying to erase the memories of Barb's death. "I miss you," she whispers, then counts "Thirty-nine, forty, forty-one..."

She bends over at the waist and brushes it from the back to the front. Head down, fighting dizziness, she strokes her hair from the base of her skull over the top of her head, the ends form a veil in front of her face. She counts out "Fifty-three, fifty-four, fifty-five..."

On the dressing table are photographs of her loved ones; her daughter, Susan, an accomplished woman, and such a beauty, her son, Charles, a warm and loving child, who is a father now. "Fifty-nine, sixty, sixty-one..."

She sits up and tosses her hair behind her. She looks at the picture of her granddaughter and remembers when she had first seen Laura let down and brush out her hair. "Grammy, what beautiful hair you have," Alicia said as she ran her hand over the hair in awe. For several years following that Alicia refused haircuts and begged her Grammy to show her how to grow out her hair. Alicia has her mother's hair, daylight yellow with no streaks of red. In the photo, Alicia is dressed in a blue dress with a white pinafore and looks exactly like Alice in Wonderland. Alicia is older now, in her teens, has a short-cropped hairdo, and is no longer interested in growing it down her back.

Laura blinks her eyes and looks again at her reflection. The auburn hair is now silver gray. The blonde highlights have faded into a dingy yellow-gray. She watches as she brushes through it. "Seventy-seven, seventy-eight, seventy-nine..." "Where have the years gone? She still feels like the young girl whose mother made her sit and brush her hair each night and recite her homework assignments; the multiplication tables, poems, songs, lines for the school play. All the years she has invested in this hair and to what end? "Eighty-nine, ninety, ninety-one..." Peter had loved her hair, but now he is gone. He told her "when I am gone, do not sit and weep, carry on Laura." She shakes her head at the memory. "Ninety-five, ninety-six, ninety-seven..."

Peter sat down one afternoon after a round of golf. He had difficulty breathing and then complained of chest pains. Fearing heart failure, she called 9-1-1 and rode along in the ambulance. They ran tests, and she prayed. Her prayers were answered; it was not a heart attack. It was not heart failure. It was not fatal, not that day. But they found cancer in his lungs and scheduled him for surgery, chemotherapy and scan after scan. He had a rare form of cancer, which they were unable to stop. "But slow growing," the oncologist said. It was debilitating to Peter. He was no longer active, and in time, he lost interest in even leaving the house.

She curtailed her social life to be with him. They would sit together and watch home movies or relive their years together through photo albums. Then after a year, he had talked about how he wanted her to help him exit with dignity. She had cried. Before he chose to take that action, he had died peacefully in his sleep.

Now she feels utterly alone. Can she go through another day like today? Monotonous. Everything the same. "Ninety-nine, one hundred." She lays the brush down. Looking at herself, she tries a smile but feels its falseness and lets her lips settle back to the straight mouth grimace that has become her norm. "Get on with it," she says to her reflection, watching her lips move. She opens the drawer and picks up the vial of morphine. She squirreled this away; enough to help Peter exit. Tonight she will go to sleep, never to wake.

The phone rings on the nightstand.

"Hello," she says.

"Mom, I'm glad I caught you. I know today is a special day for you. Can I come over?"

"Susan?"

"Mom, it's me. Sorry, it's so late but with work and the kids, please, can I come tonight?"

Laura goes back to the dressing table and places the vial and the syringe back into the drawer. Why of all days is this the day Susan calls to come over? What if she had just come and found me asleep in bed? What if it was Charley or Alicia? Laura shakes these thoughts from her head.

Lurking behind them is the harder memory to erase. The thought of it brings it back in Technicolor. Laura was eleven. She had been at a friend's house after school; her mother suggested that she go, and wait for her father to pick her up. But Laura wanted to come home early. She walked home before her father left work. She entered through the kitchen door expecting to find her mother. She was not there. Laura checked the downstairs rooms and called out, "Mom, I'm home." The house was silent, she climbed the stairs to the upper floor. Laura listened outside her mother's room. Hearing nothing, she turned the doorknob. The room was dark, drapes drawn, bed rumpled. She called out again, "Mom?" The door to the bathroom was ajar; she turned away, then turned back and pushed the door open. Her mother was there in the bathtub, submerged. Her hair was splayed about her head floating on the surface of the water.

"Mom?" Laura said and reached to shake her shoulder. "Mom!" The water was cold, her mother did not respond. Laura did not comprehend what she was seeing. She shut the door and went back to the steps outside the kitchen door. She sat there and waited until Father came home.

Tears streak Laura's cheeks. This is her worst nightmare. She asks herself why she would allow this to become her children's nightmare. She wipes her eyes and her nose on the sleeve of her flannel nightgown, then looks into the mirror. "Look here. You have got to get on with your life. Change things. You've made it a year without Peter. He told you to carry on. Don't deny your children a mother, like your mother, did."

Laura opens the drawer and removes the vial of morphine and the syringe. She drops them into the wastebasket, and picks up the scissors. She pulls a hank of hair to her shoulder, and lops it off with the scissors, letting the hank of hair fall into the basket. Then she takes another and another.

Susan rings the doorbell. She is always unsure of whether to barge into her family home or let her mother answer the door. Today would have been hard for her mother; her father's death. She knows her mother has been depressed; she and Charley have talked about it often, neither knowing how to snap her out of it. Susan and Charley know about the morphine. Their dad told them, so they had replaced the contents with saline long ago.

Laura feels lighter as she descends the stairs and opens the front door. Susan stands there with a bakery box. Susan, her daughter, has the same physical coloring as her father.

"Oh my God! Mom, what did you do to your hair?"

"Time for a change. What's in the box?"

"Lemon bars, your favorite."

"Thank you, Susan. Let's go to the kitchen. What's up with the kids?"

It Starts With

Elizabeth's blue eyes widen, her auburn curls spring out from her head like coiling rope, her hands flutter in the air like a flurry of finches. "Why?" she demands.

Her mother, Lucy, stands across the room surveying the disarray. Clothes on the floor, unmade bed, objects hurled against the wall, scrapes and dings, a broken lamp.

"Why?" the girl screeches again. "Why?"

Why indeed? her mother thinks. Why do I have to put up with your tantrums?

"Why?" the girl yells again, then bounds across the room to stand inches from her mother's face, "Why?"

Lucy does not know what set off her daughter. It could have been clothing that did not fit or could not be found. It might have been a broken crayon. It might have been anything. Lucy was down the hall when she heard the commotion and had come quickly only to witness the aftermath.

"Elizabeth, what happened here?"

Elizabeth stares at her mother, her arms are outstretched, the question "why" on her lips.

"I need you to help me understand. Can you use words? What is wrong?"

Elizabeth crumbles to the floor, tears flood her eyes. "Why?"

"Is there something you can not find? I can help you. What is it?"

Elizabeth looks at her mother. She expects an answer to her question, "Why?" Why doesn't her mother give her the answer?

Lucy picks up the clothing from the floor. She hangs the blouses, the skirts in the closet. She returns the t-shirts, the socks to their drawers. Elizabeth sits on the floor, cross-legged, crying quietly, murmuring to herself. Lucy listens trying to pick out the problem from her daughter's mumbles. She straightens the mattress on the bed, pulls the sheets and blankets taut, adjusts the comforter. She sets the pillows and the raggedy doll on the bed. So many routines learned, so many patterns to follow. If the blue pillow is on the bottom and the pink pillow on top, if the doll lay with her legs outstretched and only her head touching the pink pillow, then calm will reign. Was that the problem? Had the bed not been made to Elizabeth's satisfaction?

Elizabeth is quieting down, her breathing slower. Lucy steps around her and retrieves the lamp. It is a total loss; the shade bashed in where it hit the wall, the glass base shattered. Lucy stuffs the lamp inside a black plastic garbage bag, then kneels to pick up the broken shards of glass. One or two lamps break each year, she will shop at the thrift store and pick up another one. Elizabeth doesn't care about lamps as long as they go on at nightfall and stay lit until dawn. Was that the problem? Had the bulb burned out?

Elizabeth sits on the floor, her head drooping down, worn out. Lucy wants to go to her daughter, embrace and rock her gently, soothe her, "It'll be alright." She has been denied this all of Elizabeth's twenty-two years. Elizabeth screams at touch. "It is the way she is wired," Lucy was told. Elizabeth doesn't fit in this world, she lives inside a world where order and consistency are demanded.

Lucy wonders why this is her burden, why she doesn't have a normal child, why she is locked in this struggle day after day. She thinks of Fred, her husband, putting his hands over his ears when Elizabeth cried for hours and hours as a newborn. When Elizabeth was diagnosed autistic, when it was learned that this is the way she will be, he left. He flung the ultimatum, "Put her in a home or else." Lucy wonders if she should have agreed. Who would have looked after Elizabeth? Would it have been better not to coddle and cater to her? Would it have been better for me?

Lucy stands. The room is back in order, neat and clean. She nods to Elizabeth. "Everything is where it belongs. You can get up now."

Elizabeth raises her head and surveys the room. She lifts the dust ruffle on the bed, reaches underneath and withdraws a shoe. She clasps it her chest. Tears well in Lucy's eyes, she recognizes the shoe. It is a brown wingtip, Fred's. One he did not take when he left, though he came back saying he was missing a shoe, they couldn't find it.

Elizabeth holds the shoe, rocking gently. "Why?"

Lucy watches her daughter's frenzy rebuild. Once she gets on a tangent, there is no derailing it. She has to wait out the storm, then mop up afterward.

Elizabeth stands, offers the shoe to Lucy and demands, "Why?"

Lucy takes a deep breath, moistens her lips. She searches for words. How can she explain that her father did not want to love her, or them?

Elizabeth needs an answer. "Why?" Her mother seems broken, distant, and unable to answer this one question. Elizabeth prompts her, "It starts with because."

The Call Center

"I hate my job," my sister Darla wails, as she flops onto the bed beside me.

"You do? Why?"

"It's not the job, it's the people." She bursts into tears and flails on the bed. Her arms beat on the mattress; she pummels the pillow with her fists. "They don't care," she said.

"And you do," I said. I hold her in my arms and listen, as she tells me about her work environment. My heart goes out to her because she spent three years chasing every job that she could find, only to land this one. She knows she doesn't have a choice but to stick with it.

When the rage is spent, she turns to me. "I'm sorry."

"Don't be. Sit back, relax. You need a diversion," I tell her. "I've got an idea for a sitcom."

Imagine this. The scene is a call center; you know, little cubicles with no décor. Everything is a dingy gray color, makes you wonder if the walls were ever white. Nothing on the walls, cubicle walls same dull non-color as the walls in the room. Flooring is vinyl, cracking at the seams. There are twelve cubicles. Every cubicle is the same, a five-foot wide expanse of workspace with a flat panel display, a keyboard, and a mouse. No personal items. No pictures of the family. No awards, no plaques.

At the front of the room on the wall that all the cubicles face, there is a digital display. This focal point ticks off the time in foot-high numbers, and around that are twelve boxes showing real-time call stats. Each employee is represented in one of these boxes, calls made, leads generated, sales completed. The employees think of it as "The Scoreboard," their enemy.

The clock displays the time as 5:58 a.m. and all the scores are zeroed. The door to the room opens, and a middle-aged woman enters. She heads toward her cubicle in the back of the room, takes off her coat, carefully hangs it on the back of her chair, opens a drawer, removes the headset, and places her purse in the drawer. She adjusts the headset, plugs it into the computer and begins her day.

"Good morning," she says, "I'm Deborah with Affordable Housing Dot Com..."

The camera jumps from Deborah to the clock and fast-forwards to 8:30 a.m. The display shows that Deborah has completed twenty-two calls, and generated seven leads. Other employee stats are starting to tally. The camera pulls back to show that now eleven of the cubicles are occupied.

One employee working next to the empty cubicle leans back in her chair and says to another, "She's usually here by eight twenty.

"I know, but she's supposed to be here at eight, like me."

"Maybe she called in sick."

"Sick? Ya' got that right."

That comment unleashes snickers throughout the room. As if to punctuate that the door bangs open, and a woman wearing a faux leopard coat with her hair still in rollers storms into the room.

"Well!" she says walking to her cubicle in the center of the room. She throws out the "well" as her opening gambit, and turns in a slow circle while dropping her coat to the floor. She waits for her co-workers to look at her. Not getting much of a response, she places her hands on her more than ample breasts and says, "Lord my nipples are on fire!" Everyone looks up at her. She is dressed in blue plaid fleece pajama pants and a black satin lace camisole that is barely covering her. Getting the attention she wants, she laughs. All eyes dart back to their displays.

The camera pulls back to the wide-angle view of the room. The clock shows time moving on; stats start ticking up for everyone, except one. The camera continues in fast forward mode.

The woman in the black camisole sits, then stands, leaves the room, returns with a bowl and eats at her desk, then leaves. She later returns dressed for work in skintight jeans and a low cut red sweater. She attaches a bicycle rear view mirror to the side of her monitor. She applies her makeup; heavy on the black eyeliner, blue eye shadow and carefully adheres false eyelashes. Her black hair has been brushed and ratted up into an outdated bouffant style. When she places the headset on, it disappears into her hair, all except the microphone that juts across her left cheek. She applies bright purple lipstick, smacks her lips together and makes her first call. The clock reads 9:45 a.m.

Her employee file says her name is Rebecca James, but she wants to go by Becki with a star over the "i." On calls, though, she always refers to herself as "Lola" and has been known to launch into "Whatever Lola wants, Lola gets," as proof to her clients that she can work miracles.

The camera scans the room; her attire is out of place and inappropriate. The other employees are dressed neatly, business casual. After all they never actually meet with anyone, they just talk on the phone.

Ms. Rogers enters the room and weaves her way around the cubicles listening and taking notes in the notebook that she carries balanced on her left arm, pen in her right hand. She is the call center supervisor. She is twenty-four, fresh out of business school and totally unprepared for her job. What she lacks in confidence she tries to cover with her navy blue pantsuit and white silk tee. A single strand of pearls used to complete the ensemble, but the string broke, and the pearls dispersed across the fitness center shower room floor. She watched as two or three rolled into the drain and others floated in the puddles of water from dripping bathing suits. She didn't know their value, a graduation gift from her aunt, so she let them go.

She doesn't understand the clients or their needs; she doesn't understand her employees or how to motivate or discipline them. She has no real authority and is unaware that everyone knows it.

She prides herself on the fact that she meets with each employee once a week. As they all work different shifts so that the call center can be active in four time zones seven days a week, she schedules these one-on-ones on Wednesdays and Thursdays when all twelve employees are in the call center.

Each employee has different needs. Frank is afraid his cancer is coming back but refuses to pursue medical advice. He can confess this to Ms. Rogers, but not to his wife or physician. He recently turned sixty and was thankful to get this job after being out of work for several years, but he doesn't feel compassion toward the people who call in. He often mishandles the calls and has been known to tell them honestly, "I don't know," after which he waits patiently for them to hang up.

Margaret has been with Affordable Housing Dot Com since its inception. Her performance fluctuates, but Ms. Rogers gives no opinion. She is afraid of Margaret's seniority with the company and feels that any criticism might reflect poorly back on her.

Ms. Rogers has been with Affordable Housing Dot Com for nearly one year. She anticipates a performance review and only pushes those employees that she hired. She doesn't feel confident enough with the others, besides two of those she has hired are the top performers. She has faith that based on these two;

she will earn a merit increase, maybe a substantial bonus. Then she could replace the pearl necklace.

As she approaches Becki's desk, she becomes aware of the sound of someone eating. The employees are not supposed to have food at their desk. She has not denied them their coffee, tea, soda or water, but now snacks have crept their way onto the desks. Wait, what was that? It couldn't be that someone is blowing bubble gum and popping the bubble with a snap? She stops, and turns slowly, surveying the face of each caller. "Who is chewing gum? Gum is prohibited." It is one of the eleven "Don'ts" posted in the employee lunchroom. If there is one thing that will set off Ms. Rogers, it is chewing noisily into the phone.

It all started last Easter someone brought in a glass canister filled with jellybeans. She was going to remove it when she saw it, but Mr. Levine saw it first and commented to her how it seemed to cheer up the place.

Mr. Levine is the founder and CEO of Affordable Housing Dot Com. "He's the boss you could learn to hate," is how Ms. Rogers thinks of him. He had a credentialed reputation as a heavy hitter in the venture capital community among those she knew in grad school. Because of that she sought to work in one of his companies. Supervisor in a call center had not been her ideal choice, but she took it. It was a start she told herself and continued to tell herself. Now, however, she knows some things about Mr. Levine that make him less iconic.

And then there is his nephew, Saul Levine. Saul is the CFO, a position he earned because of a couple of accounting classes at a community college. He is full of himself. He walks around all day with his iPad in his hand, tapping on the screen, sometimes smiling, sometimes frowning, and then tap tap tapping away. She never knows if he is playing Candy Crush or doing some work. Saul likes to come into the call center and chat up Becki. Chat up, huh, she thinks more like look down at her boobs which is why he hovers over her desk asking inane questions. It never mattered what they talked about; Becki liked the attention.

It's even worse when Mr. Levine comes into the call center. Becki will stand up and stretch, her arms over her head, then lower her hands behind her back. When he is across the room and looking her way, she will bend forward at the waist, so there is no mistaking what she is showing him. He usually watches. Ms. Rogers is embarrassed by their actions and exits the room, to sit behind her desk in the windowless office on the second floor.

The employees have confided to her that they have problems working with Becki.

"She comes in her pajamas, and eats breakfast at her desk."

"She is always late."

"She cheats somehow."

Ms. Rogers diverts their concerns rather than addressing them. "We all have our differences," she says.

Margaret and Deborah share their concerns to one another, but neither told Ms. Rogers that they believe Becki and Mr. Levine are having an affair. What other reason would there be that no one ever gets on her case about all the things she does that are against the rules.

"Gum?" Ms. Rogers says as she stops beside Becki's cubicle. "Are you chewing gum?"

"Um." Becki looks up at Ms. Rogers and continues snapping her gum. She places her hand over the microphone and pantomimes "I'm on a call," but it's clear on her monitor, that she has "logged off on break."

"Dispose of the gum and let's go to my office for our weekly," Ms. Rogers says.

Becki stands, unplugs but keeps the headset on, and follows Ms. Rogers to her office.

"Sit down. Let's go over your numbers."

"Crap."

"I beg your pardon." Ms. Rogers looks at Becki. Did she really say that? How do I respond to her disrespect?

"Sorry. It's sooooo boring going over the numbers. Look, I make the calls. You can see how many calls I make."

"I do, but I'm concerned about why you are unable to achieve the conversion numbers like the other callers."

Becki leans across Ms. Rogers' desk. Her eyes get real big (if behind those lashes and all that eyeliner they could get any bigger). "I think someone is cheating the system."

"What?" This is what everyone says Becki is doing. "Why do you say that?"

"No one ever got those results before. Then you bring in these two new people and keep telling us how good they are, blah blah blah, but no one else can get those kinds of numbers, so they are cheating. There, I said it." She sits back, arms folded across her chest, a satisfied look on her face.

Ms. Rogers looks at Becki. She can't come up with a response.

"So, what are you going to do about it?" Becki asks.

"Well…I'm not sure right now, but we've been talking about recording the calls."

"That's illegal. You can't do that. I saw it on Law and Order."

"Calm down. It's not a personal call; it's business. We can, and when we do, we will learn what language is used to close the deal. Maybe we can all learn how to do our job better."

Becki stands up. "Nope, not gonna' happen. It's illegal, and I know it." She sits back down. Then opens her purse takes a piece of gum, unwraps it, pops it in her mouth and starts to chew.

"Becki, we can't allow gum chewing in the office. It sounds horrible on the phone."

"I'm too upset. I need to burn off some of this anger. I'll go to lunch now." She rises and leaves.

Ms. Rogers sits stunned.

The camera pulls back to the wide-angle view of the call center. Becki enters snapping her gum and grinning. She takes off her headset and drops it noisily on the desk, and then takes her purse and coat and announces, "I'm at lunch."

Under lowered eyelids everyone watches as she sashays out of the office, then they make comments between calls. Everyone checks their schedules and has to change their regular rotation for lunch to cover the absence of Becki. It's 10:15 a.m.

Saul sticks his head in the room and asks, "Where's Becki?"

No one answers him. In the background you hear multiple voices saying, "Affording Housing Dot Com, how may I help you."

Darla laughs "Oh goodness, that's exactly what it is like."

"Oh, then you can see the humor of it."

"Tell me more." She lays back, her tears forgotten.

The clock has now advanced to 11:30 a.m. Deborah checks her watch, even though the clock on the scoreboard is accurate. She leans back in her chair and waits for Margaret to finish her call.

"She's not back yet."

"I know."

Deborah taps her watch and Margaret nods. Deborah logs off the system and leaves the room. Margaret follows.

"I can't believe she gets away with it."

"I know. She comes in late, leaves early, takes what is now an hour lunch break when we only have half an hour..."

Deborah sighs, "I'm starving! I've been here since six. This is ridiculous."

"I know. I'm taking my lunch break with you. Let's plan that trip to Italy."

"Oh yeah, right," Deborah laughs. "The only way I'm going to be able to afford that trip is if I win the lottery."

At noon, Deborah and Margaret clear away the remnants of their lunch and go back to work. They are surprised to see Becki at her desk. She is on the phone, and they hear her.

"Oh yeah, we can certainly make that work. Yeah, we do take that into account."

Margaret and Deborah sit down, put on their headsets and roll their eyes at one another.

"Affordable Housing Dot Com, how may I help you?" Deborah says. As she listens to the caller, she looks up to the scoreboard and gasps.

Frank hears her and looks up at the scoreboard. "Damn!"

Margaret hears Frank and follows his glance to the scoreboard. The numbers are up. Becki, though she has put in less than an hour at her desk, now has logged twenty-seven calls. "There is no way!" Margaret hisses.

Becki picks up her cell phone and dials a number, her headset rings, and she answers,

"Affordable Housing Dot Com." She listens for a time, then hangs up without saying anything. Becki looks at her cell phone, selects a number, and calls; her headset rings and she says, "Affordable Housing Dot Com" and hangs up. Each time she does this, her call number advances. Margaret sits and watches. She appears dumbstruck.

At 2:30 p.m., Deborah logs off the system, disconnects her headset, replaces it in the drawer and puts on her coat and leaves. Margaret waves and Frank nods. Deborah stops at the lunchroom where Michael is sitting.

"How's it going?" she asks.

"Okay, I guess, still trying to get the hang of it."

"You'll do fine. Follow the script and tune out the drama in the call center."

"Thanks, Deborah. Good night."

Michael is the newest employee. He has only been on the job about a week. He sits right in front of Becki. She has given him a hard time. Michael is very sensitive. He is a transsexual and was born female but is in the process of transitioning to male. He looks more like a woman than a man and still has a female body but has begun hormone treatment that will lower his voice and bring on beard growth. After a year, he will be able to have sexual reassignment surgery, which will result in a hysterectomy and mastectomy. Becki teases him, she calls him Michelle and says it with a fake French accent.

Deborah has grown quite fond of Michael. One day over lunch he shared with her his spiritual connection. He is convinced that he is connected to the spirit world, and can see and hear them. He told Deborah of a long conversation with a female spirit who said she was Deborah's mother and wanted to tell her something.

Ms. Rogers steps into the lunchroom and looks at Michael, then at her watch and leaves. Michael checks the time. He has only been on his lunch break for twenty minutes; he should have another ten minutes, but panics over the way she checked her watch. He throws away his lunch and returns to his cubicle. If he can hold down this job for a full year, he will fulfill the requirement to satisfy the psychologists and be approved for surgery. He can wait it out.

Ms. Rogers is very uncomfortable around Michael. When she read the resume, it was a resume for a woman, and she had hired her thinking that she would not add to the drama, and be a good worker. But on that first day, she came dressed in Dockers slacks, a button down oxford shirt, tie, and men's black dress shoes. She asked to be called "Michael." It was the opposite of no drama, but the Human Resources manager said that all the affirmative action regulations require that no mention of Michael's transgender status can be used as grounds for dismissal.

Ms. Rogers walks through the call center and notes on her pad who is in the midst of a call and who is not on a call. She glances up at the scoreboard and notes that Deborah made over seventy calls, generated nineteen leads, and was credited with four closings.

The closest person to that many calls is...Becki. She stands there staring at the board. She knows there is no way those stats are accurate. Becki hadn't made even five calls before she went to lunch, and she has been back on the phone for barely two hours. But there are no leads, no closings. She hurries to her office and pulls up the call log on the computer. This shows all the incoming and outgoing calls for each person. It does not include the callers' phone numbers, which is a constant source of irritation. Instead, it reports only the number of calls answered by each operator. She has asked for a way other than recording the calls, to identify if the caller is active on the phone or on hold, and the duration of the call. That information is not available.

Ms. Rogers uses her personal cell phone to call into the call center. Frank answers the first call, and she learns that he doesn't know how to handle callers needing Section Eight housing. She makes another call and this time, Becki answers. Of course, she identifies herself as Lola. Ms. Rogers explains that she is moving to the city and needs affordable housing. She asks what assistance she may get from Affording Housing Dot Com. Becki smacks her gum into the receiver, and Ms. Rogers records the call. Becki surprises Ms. Rogers because she gives the appropriate answer but fails to offer the recommended referrals.

Instead, she says, "Mandy, is that you? Good one."

Ms. Rogers can't help herself. She says, "Yea, what's up?" thinking that is what one of Becki's friends would say.

"You gotta' meet me later. I'm dying to tell you about last night. Oh my gawd, you won't believe it."

"What?"

"Well, I'm at work, you know. But Mr. L, you know who I mean? He tells me to meet him at The Mark and then we have some drinks, and I tell him, he really owes me dinner for, you know, in his office..."

The camera pulls back. Ms. Roger listens intently on her phone, her face reddening in embarrassment. Becki continues talking and those sitting near her lean toward her picking up bits and pieces of the conversation. The camera pulls back further and fades on the scoreboard.

"Yep, that is what it is like. I hadn't thought about Becki and Mr. Levine. I'll keep closer tabs on those two," Darla said. "Love you sister."

"Me, too," I said.

A Question of Alarm

Last night, I was awakened by the doorbell. I opened the front door to my estranged husband.

"What?" I said when I saw it was he.

"I drove all night to be with you," he said.

I opened the door wide. Could this be true? Was he coming home to stay?

I climbed back into bed. He took me in his arms, and we made love. My heart soared, maybe, this time, he'd stay.

"Linda did you set the alarm?" he mumbled as he drifted into sleep.

His question brought me fully awake. Is that what he said or did he say, 'When did you set the alarm? Uncertain, I left the bed and sat on the sofa in the dark living room counting out the syllables.

Lin-da-did-you-set-the-a-larm

When-did-you-set-the-a-larm

Almost the same. The problem is that I am not Linda and Linda is the one he left me for. I try to convince myself that the latter version is true, that it shouldn't matter because he's here with me now.

In the morning he showers and leaves.

A Walk In The Woods

A hickory nut falls on the footpath. I kick it away, then wait. Will a squirrel scamper down and pick it up? On my right, I hear a rustling in the bushes. Something larger than a squirrel is on the move. They are breaking small twigs as they come through the underbrush. I stand as if stuck, unable to discern the path of the animal. Is it ahead or behind me?

As if on cue, dark clouds shield the sun and darkness falls quickly in this thicket of trees. How far have I come into the forest? It was a spur of the moment adventure, a walk off the beaten path to clear my mind.

It moves closer. I can hear his footfalls as they land on small rotting branches and the Snap! Snap! Snap! heightens my awareness that danger is moments away. I hear the raspy breath of a beast. I imagine that he is running with his tongue hanging out. His mighty jaw is lined with sharp daggers of teeth. My blood races faster through the chambers of my heart. My breath quickens as if to meet that of the beast. Is there only one or are there more? I listen hoping to hear it moving away but nearer it comes.

A dank odor pierces the piney smell of the air, a fetid animal scent of damp fur, and wet earth. My breakfast churns in my stomach and lurches. I am about to heave, yet I cannot move from this place and save myself.

I imagine the police finding my torn, gnawed and ravaged body. Parts of it lying here on the footpath, maybe other parts eaten or left there by the trunk of that long ago burned out tree. How long will the agony last? How long before they find me? Should I scream? Will someone come to my aid? Will it only attract the beast to me quicker? If only I could remove this force that holds me here and run. Yes, run.

I pick a spot ahead on the path that is open. That is where I need to run to. I need to run there now.

I feel the hot panting breath of the beast as it moves through the last few feet to me. My feet are stuck. I am unable to move. I throw my hands up and cover my face, I squat and turn away, as if I can hide. Only a few minutes have passed since I kicked that hickory nut that fell onto the footpath, but it feels as if a lifetime of inaction and indecision has passed.

As I cower waiting for my fate, a black animal bursts through the brush and bounds at me. Once, twice, three times, it circles around me. Then the black lab drops the red ball and waits for me to pick it up, and throw it.

Reunion

Susan didn't recognize the return address on the bright pink envelope and thought it most likely junk mail, but opened it anyway. It was an invitation to her high school reunion, the fiftieth. How could all this time have passed? She pushed it aside, but her thoughts turned to the friends she had in high school. Those friendships hadn't survived all these years. Was there anyone she wanted to reconnect with?

The reunion was a series of events planned over two days; a trip back to the high school, a wine tasting, a formal dinner. Why didn't they just recreate the junior prom held in the high school cafeteria? She had spent all day on campus decorating and preening for the junior prom, only to trudge home with no plans to attend.

The invitation sat on her desk for nearly two months; being moved from the pile of bills to the to-do file, and finally held in her hands to commit or toss. Susan sent in the registration, then sat with a mug of Southern Comfort and her high school yearbook trying to remember who had meant something to her.

When friends listened to her chatter about the upcoming reunion, most often they heard her fear that she wouldn't recognize anyone, or be recognized. That was still on her mind when the day arrived.

Susan received two messages on the day of the reunion. One canceled the tour of the school due to a conflict; the other announced that those already headed to the school would meet up at the local burger joint. What was the name then? Tim's Drive-In? Today it's Bell Street Bakery. It was only two blocks away from the school. She checked her hair, applied another layer of lipstick, smiled at herself and remembered her friend's advice that her smile was her best asset.

Inside, she saw that the bakery was more of an eatery than just cupcakes and cookies. The lights were dim but the afternoon sun was streaming in. There were some teens, girls with piercings, boys with spiky hair, lounging around tables and her hopes of a glass of courage were diminished. Then she saw the backroom with a neon light advertising beer on tap. That looked promising, and she made her way across the sticky vinyl floor through the maze of tables to the bar. It was easy to see that tables had been pushed together, people her age sitting, talking and gesturing. She didn't recognize anyone and rather than stand there gawking, she turned toward the bar and took the first empty stool. Her back was now to the group. If no one had recognized her when she came in, they weren't going to recognize her now, but she could listen to their conversation. She ordered a rum and coke; it seemed to fit the high school theme.

While sipping her drink, she heard one woman talking about decorating the cafeteria for the prom. She wondered if that woman would recognize her as one of her compatriots. She tried to catch a look at the speaker without making it obvious, but whether she turned right or left, she could not see her. Curiosity got the best of her, and she walked into the crowd. She took a good look at the gray-haired lady laughing about making crepe paper flowers. Had they made crepe paper flowers for the prom? That is not what she remembered. What was the theme? Something cheesy like "under the sea." That was it – "Under The Sea." They hung row after row of lime green and blue-green streamers from the ceiling to the floor on all four walls of the cafeteria to create that underwater scene. She looked over the faces of those around the tables and despite her hours of study with the yearbook, she was unable to identify any of them.

She felt someone standing beside her. She looked and found a handsome man smiling at her.

"I was wondering if you would remember me," he said.

She smiled back. "I'm here for the reunion."

"I know. I saw your name on the list."

"There's a list?"

"Of course there's a list. Do you remember this group?" He pointed to the table where the gray-haired woman was still talking about crepe paper flowers though others were talking about the pregnancies that followed the regional championship that year.

Susan shrugged. "Not really."

"Same blah blah like high school," he said. "Let's go catch up in a quieter place."

He led her across the room into a booth in the back corner. He signaled the waiter, and suddenly there were two drinks on the table.

"I remember, rum and coke," he said.

She nodded. *How does he know anything about me and I know nothing of him? In fact, what is his name?*

"So, what have you been up to? You still live around here?"

She began to answer his questions, and there were a lot of them. "What happened after high school? Did she go to college? Kids? Was she a grandmother? If so, she was the prettiest grandmother he had ever met."

One rum and coke at the bar, then two, at the booth. She was feeling loose and woozy. *Wasn't there supposed to be food?*

"Do they serve food here?" she asked.

"Hungry?" he asked.

"Starving," she said.

He waved over a waiter and took the menu. He looked it over, lowered it and smiled at her. "You won't believe the special today. Your favorite."

That was creepy. She felt that she had put herself in jeopardy and not the game show. This guy whose name she didn't know was buying her drinks and telling her he knew her favorite on the menu. *Where was this going?*

She rose, "I have to use the bathroom."

He slid out of the booth and offered his hand to help her. As she moved past him heading for the restroom, he whispered, "Meatloaf."

It is my favorite, she thought. *How does he know?* In the restroom, she washed her hands, fluffed her hair and reapplied her lipstick. *Am I in trouble here or just feeling uncomfortable? Who is he?*

A woman exited the stall and smiled at her. "Lucky you. There are quite a few girls who came back just to see how Adrian Johnson had aged, and you've got him all to yourself."

"Yes," she said. Yes to the fact that he was a handsome man and in good physical shape.

The woman dried her hands and left.

Adrian Johnson? She asked herself. *Who is Adrian Johnson?*

"You're back, and the food is here. Just in time," he said, sliding into the booth beside her.

"It looks great," she said, looking down at a steaming platter with two slices of meatloaf, catsup, mashed potatoes and green beans. She picked up a green bean with her fingers and bit into it.

"Ouch," he said. "Looks like you like to bite."

She picked up another, and snapped her teeth down hard on it, watching him.

He laughed, "Oooh, still a live wire."

Who does he think I am? I was never a live wire in high school.

He scooted over closer to her, moved the fork to his right hand, and laid his left hand on her knee. "Ambidextrous," he said.

"What?" She knew what the word meant, but why say it now? And his hand on her knee, it was warm, and it felt nice, but this wasn't right. *Too soon?*

When their plates were cleared, he talked of taking her dancing and back to his place. She wasn't tracking the conversation well. There was a lot of noise in the bar, and that group of people had expanded. She wondered if they were still talking about crepe paper flowers.

She felt tired, very tired, and realized she could fall asleep if she just let her eyes close. *Could I sleep for a minute and be refreshed or do I need an eight-hour recharge?*

"I don't know about dancing," she said.

"I was being polite," he said. He moved his hand from her knee up her thigh, then leaned in and kissed her. Kissed her right on the lips. She didn't do anything but let him. His lips were warm and tasted of rum and coke. There was a strength there she liked.

"Let's go," he said. "My engine is running and looks like you are revving up."

Susan reached for her purse. This felt just like high school. That awkward date when he wanted one thing, and she wanted another. But this wasn't high school, she was sixty-eight years old, and so was he.

"I need some fresh air," she said and headed to the door. She put her hand in her purse jingling for the keys, not sure what she was going to do. As they walked out, some one in the crowd shouted out.

"Just like the old days."

"Some things never change," said another.

"You go Johnson..." said another man. At that there was cheering.

"All the way to the end zone," some one shouted.

Susan could feel the instant heat of embarrassment climb up her throat and blaze her cheeks. There was something reminiscent about their taunts.

Adrian was beside her, "Let's take my car," he said. "I don't want you that far away from me."

She looked at him. Was he for real? "I'm sorry, but I don't think you mean me. I...I don't know you?"

Facing her, he put his hands on her shoulders; he stood nearly a foot taller than she. "You do know me. I know you."

"But..." There was something familiar in his stance, but who was he? Why didn't she remember? She wanted to run, and she wanted to stay. It was nice to have someone want to drive you, want to take the lead, but it felt dangerous.

"Here," he said. He cupped her elbow and led her to a white Camaro.

"Do you recognize her?"

She looked around. "Who?"

"The car, silly," he said. "New paint job but same car as high school."

"You still drive the same car?"

"Just take it to car shows, but thought you'd appreciate it tonight."

"Tonight?" Susan recognized that she was repeating what he said. She was feeling lost, but willing to go along. It felt better than fighting it. He opened the passenger door, and she slid in.

"Your right," she said.

"Of course," he said and started the engine. "Right about what?"

"The car. I like it."

He smiled and pulled into traffic.

She leaned her head back and watched his hands on the steering wheel. The oncoming headlights glinted off the gold ring on his left hand. She twisted an identical ring on her own hand, then laughed.

"I'm back," she said. "I can't believe I didn't know who you were."

"You're doing fine now," he said. "The doctor said you might suffer some memory loss after the stroke last month. You're getting better."

The Red-Winged Hawk

Some feelings are universal, such as a mother's ache for the loss of a child. It is impossible to weigh that pain or to compare a mother's loss whether the child is young or older. Always to the mother, it will be her child. She blames herself over and over again about what she could not control. She creates rules and boundaries and tries to imagine a world where the child is still alive. Maybe she pleads with God to take her instead and change the course of time. Years pass, but that ache of loss is never out of reach.

Geri still cried when she stood at the kitchen sink and washed dishes. Here with the water running, Bud can't hear her, and she is safe to sink into the depth. The entry point begins with "If only I had done something different with him when he was little. If only I could have known that this is what would happen. If only I could have prevented it."

I have waited for the knock on my door or the phone call, "Ma'am we're sorry, but your son was killed today in an accident." It would involve some daring feat dealing with a wheeled vehicle, and I have long set myself that when this happens, I must accept that he went doing what he loved. I remember him standing in the bathroom washing the road from his skin – raw, pink, tender, and scarring.

"Let's go to the hospital," I said.

"Naw, mom, I'll be okay."

Even now, so many years later, I still wince at the memory.

What is it that we, the mother, grieve over? Is it the potential we felt the child could reach, the loss of one we loved dearer than any other? I remember the despair I felt at the loss of the yet unborn child That day, lying on the couch, my face into the pillow to muffle my sobs, I traveled the road of loss.

Geri felt the same despair when her son at the age of thirty-two, took his own life. She could imagine the pain he felt when his wife left him. She felt that pain when after eight children, her husband divorced her. He was done with her. But she had not wanted to die. Secretly she had wanted to kill him and his young girlfriend. While she knew how it felt to be abandoned and discarded, she did not know why her son chose death. "If only he called me," she thought, and she thought of all the things she would have said to him.

The dishes were clean. The sink was scoured. The windowsill had been wiped dry. She had no more excuse to stand at the sink, yet the water still ran, masking her sobs. Her tears dripped down the drain. She looked out the window, beyond the patio, and over the fence. She watched a bird land, and it looked directly at her. She watched and recognized it as a hawk, a red-winged hawk. A bird of prey that is as likely to be preyed upon by a larger bird. One with a quirky habit of cocking its head, left then right, to be sure that it was safe. But this red-winged hawk landed on her fence and stood stock still, and looked intently at her. Not at her kitchen window, but through the glass, and at her.

She turned off the water absently, not breaking her contact with the bird. A thought flitted across her mind, "Mom, I'm alright now." She narrowed her eyes and watched the bird, which watched her. "Really Mom, don't cry over me. I'm okay now." And her despair lifted.

It was out of her control; she just didn't feel sad anymore. It was as if David had spoken to her. She smiled a weak smile, a release of the pain she had been feeling. She breathed an audible sigh. The bird cocked his head at her. She cocked her head back; the bird lifted off the fence, and flew away.

Bud came in from the garden and walked over to embrace her as she stood drying her hands. She was still looking at the fence.

"Everything okay hon?"

"Yes, it's going to be okay," she said and smiled.

Shoe Wars

"It has to stop," my husband, Frank said.

"What? What has to stop?" I said. I was sitting on the bed wiggling out of my dress. I had already unfurled the pantyhose, and they hung at my ankles. The dress off, I stood and laid it out to check for any stains or signs of wear, then hung it on the hanger. I was still waiting for an explanation but stepped around him to enter my closet. "Whatever are you talking about Frank?" I asked.

He stood in the doorway of my walk-in closet, hands spread, lips set. "This has to stop." He stepped aside, and I saw that he had found my cache.

On the floor were my shoes, not just the ones he knew about, but my cherished beauties. The fury that beset him was displayed in the way he had flung them.

I knelt down, drawing the shoes toward me, righting the ones that had fallen, reuniting the pairs.

"Can you explain this to me?" He said, kicking at the toe of my sapphire blue Michael Kors pump.

I looked at him. First at his belt buckle, the Smith and Wesson one he most treasured, since I was kneeling. Then I rose and saw his red-black plaid flannel shirt. Taking a deep breath, I raised my eyes to his. We stood eye-to-eye, staring at each other; questions danced in our eyes.

"Why all the shoes?"

"Why were you looking for them?"

"What is wrong with you?"

"What is wrong with you?"

"This is beyond obsessive."

"What about your tools? Your fishing gear? Your stupid model trains!"

Words were not necessary. This conversation had played out before. I surveyed the disarray. The Jimmy Choo's lying haphazard out of their box, the MiuMiu's tossed like yesterday's newspaper and my wedding shoes. I sighed.

"Really Frank, we have to do this again?"

The look in his eyes changed, the anger replaced with disgust.

"You have a problem. I'm not sure I want to be part of it anymore."

He turned and stormed out. I heard the front door slam. This was the first time our Shoe Wars had gone this far. Usually, we yelled, pouted, and then made up.

I picked up the wedding shoes. There is three pair. All custom dyed the same off-white cream to match my wedding dress. For the church, I wore a very classic low heeled, open-toed pump, a sexier stiletto version of the same open-toe design to wear at the reception, and a strappy sandal version to wear to the after-party for dancing the night away. All only worn once, our wedding day, now six years ago. I was keeping them for our twenty-fifth anniversary.

I slipped each pair of shoes into its cloth bag, then into its box and stacked the boxes back into their resting places; I wanted to restore order.

Our first disagreement occurred shortly after I moved in with him.

"What the heck do you need all these shoes for?" he asked.

"Well, these are to you entice you to seduce me," I said holding the candy-apple red Jimmy Choo's.

He blushed and said, "I like those."

Then I picked up the black sandals I wore the first time we had sex and reminded him about that night.

"Oh yes, I remember those."

It was more than a year after our wedding when he raised the topic again. This time was now known as the First of the Shoe Wars. He opened the Nordstrom bill.

"How the hell did you manage to spend a thousand dollars on clothes in one month?"

"Let me see that." I snatched the bill and examined it. Mental note to self, don't tell him this is all about two pairs of shoes. "It's not a thousand dollars. It's only eight hundred, and this is because I have to keep up my work wardrobe. I have to present a professional appearance. You can't work in a real estate office and look like you can't afford the million-dollar house you are selling. I can't go in jeans and flannel shirts." He worked in the construction business and other than a rare client meeting, he was always dressed in the same thing, blue jeans, and a flannel shirt. I had begun to refer to it as his "lumberjack costume." At first he laughed, but lately, I could tell that it smarted when I said it. But I didn't stop.

As we got ready for bed that night, I caught him contemplating my shoes in the closet. It was my closet; he used the other closet in the hall. He seemed obsessed with my shoes. There was a pile of them kicked off, haphazard. Easy for me to retrieve when I'm dressing. The pile filled the space under the hanging dresses, and slacks for the entire length of the closet, Looking at that was enough to revive his anger.

"Really Kris. Why do you need so many shoes? There are at least five different pairs of black heels. Even if you have to have a pair in every color, why would you need more than one pair in any color?"

I glanced at him and shrugged. "Some are higher than others, open-toed for summer, closed toe for winter or business meetings, straps, no straps. It just is."

I spat out my toothpaste to punctuate the end of the discussion.

But I thought about the twenty or so pairs of boots that are boxed on the shelf and the thirty pairs of sandals in the summer collection under the bed. He hadn't looked at the back of the closet door where a hanging shoe organizer with pockets held my running shoes, cross trainers, aerobic shoes, hiking boots, and slippers. That was another sixteen pairs or was it twenty-four?

Sadly, there was Shoe Wars Two, and Shoe Wars Three, before our third wedding anniversary. I bought him the model train locomotive he had been ogling at the train show and kept it hidden from him until our anniversary. I thought he would be thrilled. He held it in his hands and looked at me.

"I thought we said no more gifts 'til we get these credit cards paid off?"

"I think I bought it before we agreed on that." I backed up a step. This wasn't going how I had planned.

"I didn't get you anything. I thought we agreed."

"It's okay," I said, but I wanted him to surprise me. I stepped away, blinking tears.

"Don't get me wrong. I like this, but I would be happier if you could get rid of some of the shoes, and not buy more."

We celebrated our third anniversary: he went on a hunting trip; I hired a contractor while he was gone. I took all of my shoes out of their hiding places and assessed them. I sorted them by work vs. not work, then by seasons, then by color. I tried on every pair and pranced in front of the mirror. I matched them to dresses and suits in the closet. I could find no reason to discard any. Every pair of boots and high-heels had its original box. The slippers and athletic shoes hung in their pouches. The sandals lounged in the plastic carrier under the bed. I slept curled in the bed while visions of my cherished shoes danced in my head. I despaired over what to do. I did not want another Shoe War.

I awoke at three in the morning and realized the perfect solution. I went into the closet and examined and measured. Scott, a friend of a friend who had done some amazing storage designs came at noon on Saturday. I showed him what I wanted, and he measured and tapped the walls and thumped around.

Finally, he declared, "It can be done."

"And you can be all done by Wednesday?"

"Yikes, that'll be a challenge."

"It has to be."

"Okay." He agreed.

When Frank came home, I met him at the door with a hug, and he responded with a kiss.

"You missed me?" I asked.

"Of course I did."

"I want to show you something. I want you to know I love you, Frank." I took him by the hand into the laundry room where a cardboard box sat, filled to the brim with shoes. "All of these are going to the charity shop tomorrow. I've done some re-organizing."

"Oh babe," he said. It felt like the peace talks were a success, and I hoped that we were well beyond the cease-fire.

Later over lunch, my best friend Patty listened and asked, "So, what did you do? I can't see you actually tossing any of your shoe inventory."

"I have a three-pronged plan. First, Scott opened up all the walls between the studs and created shoe storage. All of the panels are flush with magnetic catches so that you can't even tell it has been done. I have fifty pairs of shoes stored where you can't see them. I only keep twelve pairs of shoes in plain sight in the closet."

"Genius."

"Next, I went to Goodwill and bought shoes to fill the box. I knew Frank wouldn't look for name brands, so he'd just accept that they were mine."

"Well, you bought them, so they were yours."

"Exactly!"

"That's two, what's the third?"

"Well, Shoe Wars always happens when credit card bills arrive."

"So…you are not going to buy more shoes? I don't think that's it."

"I opened a new bank account, got a new credit card; it comes to the office. I have ten percent taken out of my paycheck for "expenses" and deposited into the new account. Frank won't see the change in income or spending. If I can keep the shoes orderly, he won't suspect a thing."

"Wait! How do you explain bringing new shoes home?"

"Really? You've met Frank, right? My mother taught me this one."

"What?"

"When she bought a new dress she slipped it into a dry cleaner bag in the trunk of her car and then hung it in her closet. My dad never saw 'new clothes' only those that had been 'dry-cleaned.'

"And?"

"If Frank should ever say, 'Honey are those new?' I just say, 'these old shoes? I had new heels put on,' or 'I got them polished.'"

"It's perfect. I think we should celebrate with dessert."

The fourth anniversary and the fifth anniversary came and were celebrated without any more Shoe Wars. Scott came back and put in attic storage in my closet so that I could rotate "stock." I kept just a dozen shoes out in the open and always kept it neat and clean.

But after Frank stormed out, he didn't come back. We both seemed to hold up licking our wounds. Monday night I called Patty and told her that Frank wanted a divorce. She suggested dinner to console me.

"What happened?"

"He found me out." I was in shock all day; I was ready to wail.

"How? I thought you had everything hidden, under control?"

"Two things." I held up two fingers and began to cry.

"Let's get a bottle of wine and then you can tell me the whole story."

"Thanks." The waiter opened the bottle, poured a taste and passed it to Patty; she sniffed it. I sniffled and watched her sip the wine.

The waiter filled her glass, then poured mine. He looked at me, his eyes full of concern or pity? I was a cliché, middle-aged woman crying her eyes out in the bar.

"First, I made the huge mistake of agreeing to be in a fashion show at the Lady's Auxiliary. Pam is helping out and begged me to pull out my most exquisite shoes and well, let's face it. What fun are they having hiding in the attic?"

"But Frank...."

"Frank never goes to those things, and who'd of thought they were going to do a story with all those photos of me in my shoes."

"Is that what did you in?"

"Not really." I took a gulp of wine. "It was my mouth, my ego, my stupidity."

"What do you mean?"

"They asked me about my shoes, and I bragged. I embellished the total number just a bit. I ran off the names; Giuseppe Zanotti, Michael Kors, Manolo Blahnik, Louis Vuitton, Gucci, Stuart Weitzman, Brian Atwood...."

"You have a pair of Atwoods?" Patty leaned across the table, one hand on her wine glass, the other on her heart.

"Yes." I delighted in really having Patty's attention. "I can't believe I never showed them to you."

"How much? I hate to ask, but I have salivated over those shoes in fashion magazines. Really you have a pair?"

"Remember last spring when I went to Palm Springs for that real estate conference? I shopped the local thrift stores and found them. I picked them up for less than a hundred dollars, and you would never know they weren't brand new."

"Maybe they weren't."

"I know, such a prize."

"But Frank saw the article? How?"

"Somebody posted it to Facebook, and someone in his office made a joke about the lady with three hundred pairs o shoes. He probably was relieved to think that someone else had a crazy wife, but then he saw it was me. He came home hell bent on proving that I was lying about the shoes. He must have stormed into my closet and moved things around. When he moved my scarves, he saw the pull down for the attic trap door, and there are all those boxes up there. He probably threw a shoe at the wall, and the damn door swung open, so he found all those shoes too. I don't think he pulled out the bins under the bed, though."

"Why is this such a sticking point with him? I guess if you're not running him into debt, what do some shoes matter?"

"He says it's the principle. I told him I had it under control, and I was lying. I was hoarding. I was going on as I was before but not being truthful with him. He said I need to make a choice, him or the shoes."

"What did you do?" She put her hands over her eyes. "Oh, Kris don't tell me, no tell me."

"I don't like ultimatums. I said 'I chose the shoes.'"

"And what happened?"

"He stared at me in disbelief, then he shrugged his shoulders and stormed out of the house. That was last Friday, and I got the divorce papers delivered to my office today."

"What are the terms? Are you going to contest it? At least you don't have any kids."

I tapped my glass, and she poured the last of the bottle. "Do you want to know what he wants?" I gulped half down.

"He probably wants the house and half of everything you own."

"No, he says I can have the house as long as I take over the mortgage."

"Wow, that's generous. What about your 401(k)?"

"He keeps his, I keep mine," I cried, my voice cracked, a sob escaped.

"Kris, what is it?"

"He gets all those things he brought into the marriage. I can have all the furniture..."

"What? What is the bastard asking for?"

"He wants half of the shoes!" I finished off the glass.

"What? C'mon what is he going to do with them?"

"He's being mean," I sobbed.

"Maybe you can let some of them go. Styles change."

"No, you don't understand."

"What?"

"He's only asking for the right shoes."

Forgetful

Marge woke to the smell of bacon. *Bacon?* she thought. *Why would Ben be cooking bacon today?*

She pulled on the sweatshirt at the end of the bed, and slipped her bare feet into the fur-lined boots by the door, and headed to the kitchen. On the way, she noted that the dog, Charlie, was not in his usual spot by the pot-bellied stove. *Curious,* she thought.

In the kitchen, smoke hung over the stove, the bacon long past crisp in the black iron skillet. "Damn," she breathed and pulled the pan off the burner. The back door was open, the chill of fresh snow blew in. She braced herself for the cold and stepped out onto the stoop. "Ben," she called. Hearing no response, she tried the dog, "Charlie, here Charlie boy."

As far as Marge could see, there was a blanket of white and one set of tracks going from the stoop into the woods at the back of the yard. One set of man-sized boot prints and one set of yellow lab prints alongside.

She went back inside, closing the door behind her, and stoked the fire in the stove. He hadn't added any wood this morning, but he'd cooked the bacon. "There's no figuring to that man no more, " she muttered. "Guess I'll go find him."

Ben had turned eighty-one this past spring, and almost overnight he had become forgetful. He had been a person given to daydreaming, but now he was a person with a bad memory which was confirmed by Doc Perkins, and getting worse every day. "Alzheimer's," the doctor had said, "Old Timers" she had heard.

She traced her steps back to the bedroom and stepped out of the boots. She pulled on wool socks, flannel lined work pants, a wool sweater over the sweatshirt, and laced up the boots. She took her winter coat off the hook and pulled on gloves and a hat; then saw Ben's winter coat hung on the hook. *Goodness,* she thought, *he's out there freezing. I'd better find him quick.*

At the kitchen door there was a chalkboard, useful when there were children, hardly used anymore. But today there was something written there.

"Enjoy the bacon. Gone for coffee."

"What the....?" She puzzled over the message and then heard Charlie at the door. *Silly me,* she thought, *all is well, here they are now.* She pulled open the door, and Charlie stood there shivering, barking, and turning in circles. This was his way to get her attention. There was something wrong.

"What's wrong boy? Where's Ben?" She ran her hands over his coat, pushing off the snow, and looking into the furthest reaches of the yard for signs of Ben. "Let's go, Charlie," she said hoping he would stop barking and lead her to him. But he clung back at the door, barking and turning in circles. Marge followed the prints in the snow that took her out past the garage, past the woodshed, past the shop where Ben used to spend hours woodworking. There were no lights on inside, but she checked the door anyway; locked, secure against the cold and animals. She kept moving, though. The wind was whipping the icy snow at her face. She pulled the collar of her coat up until it overlapped with the hat; she kept her head down as she moved further away from the warmth of the house. She wondered what the note on the chalkboard meant. *Why would he come this way for coffee? Hadn't she just gone out to the store to buy coffee the other day?* They only had bacon once a week and didn't they just have it yesterday?

As she walked, she placed her feet along beside the boot prints in the snow and marveled at how perfectly she matched the gait. Ben was so much taller than she, she felt that she had had to run to keep up with him. But now, they seemed to be locked in the same steps, and their boots seemed similarly sized. *That's curious,* she thought.

Marge stopped, stamped her right boot alongside one of Ben's boot prints. Seeing them as identical, she picked up her right foot and set it into Ben's print. *A perfect match*, she thought, *why would he go out in my boots? His feet are so much bigger than mine*. She looked down again at her boots and wiggled her toes. *Am I wearing his boots?* Wiggling her toes confirmed that these were her boots and not his.

Charlie was running circles around Marge and barking to get her attention. He had his leash in his mouth and dropped it at her feet. She picked it up, hooked it to his collar and let him lead her back to the house.

Inside, she and Charlie huddled around the stove to warm themselves. Marge could still smell the burnt bacon in the air, and that made her want a cup of coffee. When she came into the kitchen to feed Charlie, she recognized the handwriting on the chalkboard as her own. *Maybe Ben is not the only one who is getting forgetful,* she thought. With a hot cup of coffee, she went back to the parlor and sat in the chair by the stove.

On the table was a pile of sympathy cards that she suddenly noticed and with that memory came the flood of tears once more.

The Exciting World of Real Estate

On a blustery morning in early March, he rode into town. He pushed open the door and stood surveying the room. He was tall and wiry and sported a gray ponytail under his cowboy hat. He had bright blue eyes and a genuine nature that made me invite him to take a seat. I was on the desk in the real estate office. That means I am the first agent up to meet with anyone walking or calling in.

"Good morning, how may I help you?" I ask delighted to start my shift with a prospective client.

"Well, now, I've got some questions about a piece of property," he said. I detected a slight Texan drawl.

"Take a seat, let's get you some answers. Which property are you interested in?"

"It's the cornfield east of here."

"The cornfield?" I'm not sure which field he is talking about as it is March and all fields are fallow. I log onto the computer.

As he tries to explain, I spread a map out on the desk and point to one area after another, until he agrees that this is indeed the one. He places his finger on a large plat of land and emphatically taps it. "This is the one!"

"That is a partially built out subdivision. Are you interested in building it out?

"No. That's not the cornfield then."

I move on to the next parcel. "To the East, this is another subdivision that I believe has only two of its lots built."

"Yes, that must be it. I want to make an offer."

A similar sized property recently sold for over two million dollars. I am thinking about the commission. I tell him there are several properties, and a local company owns them. He asks to meet with them. I call their agent and set up a meeting for the next afternoon. The calculator in my head is still trying to place the decimal point accurately; this is a going to be a huge commission.

"Let's look at the comparables," I suggest.

"The what?" he says.

My stomach flips. "Have you thought about what you will offer?"

"Oh sure, that's all taken care of." He leans back in the chair and hooks his thumbs into the virtual suspenders he apparently thinks he's wearing.

"Then should we write up the offer?"

"Of course. Have you got some coffee?" he asks.

"Of course." I jump up and get him a cup of coffee and bring back a packet of sugar and one of creamer. I set them down in front of him.

I plop into my seat and then, he asks, "Do you have a donut or Danish?"

"Sorry, not today."

"Oh well," he says as he slurps his coffee.

"What name will you take the property in?"

"My name."

"What it is?"

"Oh, Walter A. Burnside."

"Address?"

"Well, I haven't exactly got one right now."

I look up from the keyboard. I am beginning to think that I should have done the paperwork before I called and set up the meeting.

"I'm new here and am staying with my girlfriend. (He winks at me.) I'll be looking to buy my own place just as soon as we get this property sewn up."

"Perhaps you'll want to open a post office box in the interim or use your current address," I suggest.

"Well, now that's an idea."

"Let's fill in the other blanks; we'll come back to that. Phone number?"

He pulls out a flip phone and stares at it. "Confound it. I have one, but heck if I can ever find the number."

"Here." I reach across the desk, take the phone and look up the number. I type it in, write it down, and hand it to him. "I've written it down on the back of my business card. Now you'll have it."

He looks at the card, then back at me, making me wonder whether or not I look like my photo and tucks it into his shirt pocket.

I work through the rest of the document, asking questions along the way and for the most part get the answers I am accustomed to. When I reach the financing page, I ask, "Will this be a cash purchase or will you finance it?"

"Don't worry about that, we've got that covered."

"This is for your benefit. I need to know to make the offer as accurate as possible."

"It's all arranged with Wells Fargo."

"Will it be a conventional loan? How much earnest money and how much of a down payment are you making?"

He stands, apparently upset by my questions.

"Would you like me to call over to Wells Fargo and speak with the loan officer? I know him." I say.

"No, no that won't be necessary."

"But I need to complete this for the offer. You do want to make the purchase, yes?" I hear myself going into kindergarten talk. The commission dollars are slipping away.

He sits back down. He fidgets in the chair. He picks up the pen on my desk and begins clicking it. Over and over. Click Click Click.

"As I said, this is all worked out with Wells Fargo. I am part owner of a lodge up in Alaska where I'm from. It's all worked out."

"I'll print out the offer so we can go over it," I say and send it to the printer. There are about twenty pages in all with the legal descriptions of the property and ancillary documents.

The door opens, and one of our agents enters the office. I glance up and she gives me a funny look and stares back at the client sitting before me. She walks through to her office. I am not sure what that look meant. I stop at her office while I am picking up the papers at the printer.

"Nina? What was that about?"

"Close the door."

I shut the door and got the feeling that she was going to tell me she is already working with this guy and I have no right to any commission.

"That's Walter Burnside, right?"

"Yes."

"He came in two days ago and wanted to go see a house. I took him in my car, and while we looked at two houses, he became rude, belligerent. I caught him going through the cupboards, you know, eating cookies and snacking. I told him that was unacceptable. Then he asked me to take him to his place so he could pick up his things. He said that his girlfriend had thrown him out. He directed me to a shack, no it's a shed in a field. He retrieved a couple of duffle bags and told me to drop him off at the Country Lodge. He's not viable. Get rid of him."

There was no reason for Nina to make this up. I stopped at the front desk and handed him the papers. "Look these over and I'll be right back." I went to my office and called Jim Simmons at Wells Fargo.

"Jim, I've got Walter Burnside...."

"He's a loser. Tell him to leave."

"But he said...."

"Look, he's been all over town telling people that we are working together. As far as I can tell, he hasn't got any money, or any assets and everything he says is a lie."

I go back to the front office. Mr. Burnside is making himself another cup of coffee and looking for something in the cupboards.

"May I help you?" I asked.

"Could use a donut or something along with this coffee," he said.

"Did you have a chance to look over the offer?"

"No, but I'm sure it's all right."

"The next step would be for you to go to the bank, Wells Fargo, did you say, and get a certified check for the earnest money. Then we'll be ready for the meeting tomorrow. Does that sound okay?"

He shakes his head. "No, I'm not doing any earnest money."

"Mr. Burnside, in making a substantial offer like this, you will need to provide some good faith that you are going to go through with the purchase."

The phone rings. I say, "Excuse me" to Mr. Burnside, and "How may I help you?" to the caller.

I watch Mr. Burnside collapse back into the chair and put his hand over his heart. He sets the cup on the desk and slumps in the chair.

"Good God. I heard you have Walter Burnside in your office. Are you working with him?"

"Yes, hold for a minute," I said into the phone and then turned to Mr. Burnside. "Mr. Burnside, perhaps you would like to go into the conference room where we can discuss this and finalize it? I'll ask the receptionist to go next door and buy you some pastry. Okay?"

He rises and follows her into the conference room. I pull a five-dollar bill from my wallet and ask her to get the food.

"Thanks for holding, yes I am working with him," I say into the phone.

"I took him out yesterday. He wrote an offer to purchase on that house I have listed on Maple Street, low-balled it and wrote a hundred dollar earnest money check. The seller had her car up for sale. He looked at it and wrote her a check. He took the signed off pink slip and drove it off. "

"He says he's banking with Wells Fargo..."

"Another crock. In fact, he called the cops on Jim over at the bank when he asked him to leave the office. Told the police Jim is dealing heroin."

"So, there's no real business to be done here?"

"After he wrote those checks he asked me to have coffee so we could talk about this big purchase he is about to make. We go to that new fancy diner, and I order coffee. He orders coffee and the big breakfast. When the bill comes, he shoves it across the table to me and says. 'I'm buying a house from you. You can buy me breakfast.' I did, and today both his checks bounced."

"Oh..."

"And I'm not the only Realtor® in town that he has been working with."

The receptionist is back with a box of chocolate glazed donuts. I take the donuts and get another cup of coffee. As I hand Mr. Burnside a napkin, he digs into the donuts, and the phone rings in the conference room.

"Good morning, how may I help you?

"It's Jim at Wells Fargo. I just heard that there is a warrant for his arrest. Is he still with you? Can you keep him there for five more minutes?"

"Yes, goodbye."

I watch Mr. Burnside as he takes the last donut from the box. The receptionist knocks once, enters, and hands me a piece of paper.

The note reads: "Nina filled me in. I called the Country Lodge. Mr. Burnside is not a guest there but arrives every morning at six o'clock to drink their coffee and eat their guest breakfast. He hid his duffle bags there, and Nina noticed them out at the curb with the police when she drove by. Be careful."

I hear the sirens; so distract Mr. Burnside by going back to the Finance Addendum where he can see there are several blanks. He becomes agitated again and pounds his fist on the desk." I don't need to tell them any of this. I have the authority from the city to buy this land and turn it back to its natural habitat."

As if on cue, the police come in and escort Mr. Burnside from the building. As news spreads through the small town, several more agents call to tell me their tales.

"I drove him around all one afternoon, and he wanted to offer half of what the asking price was for at least a dozen homes. He wanted me to write offers on all of them."

"He apparently got into an argument with the taxi driver (we only have one in our town) and refused to pay. The cab driver drove off with his belongings, so he claimed that the cab driver robbed him."

"I called the hunting lodge in Alaska that he said he owned. He has never been an owner though he once worked there for a short time as a guide. In fact, he was such a nuisance there, the owner bought him a one-way ticket to Miami and put him on the plane."

What happened?"

The flight connected through Seattle.... he got off the plane."

"He went to the restaurant next door to our office after he had me write up an offer. When they brought him the bill, he faked a heart attack. Apparently, that is the not the first fake heart attack he has had here. Oh, and he never came back and signed the offer I prepared for him."

I called and canceled the appointment that I made and shred the documents. I cleaned up the desk and sighed over the now evaporated commission that would have set me financially for the rest of the year.

"Next" is the most important word for any real estate agent to use, because if not this deal, there's always the next one.

It's quiet until the end of my shift at five o'clock when an elderly and slightly disheveled woman walks in.

"How may I help you?"

"Oh," she sighs as she sits down opposite me. "I'm paying cash and I want to buy a house, but first I have to escape from the home."

Lemon Pie

I set my fork down and pushed back from the table. He said it was the best dinner ever. I smiled at the compliment and pulled the lemon meringue pie from the refrigerator.

He watched me and as I brought it to the table. He stood up, put his hand on the back of my head, and shoved my face into the pie. I had labored all morning making sure the meringue was stiff, thicker than the lemon filling, and perfectly browned on the tips. Tears stung, but something in me snapped.

He fell back into his chair laughing, the whiskey ruling his actions.

I stood tall, licked my lips and without wiping the pie off my face said, "This is the best pie ever!"

He started to laugh, then the mean streak took over. He rose, fists pumping, but I pushed the chair in his path and ran out the back door. I pulled up by t-shirt and wiped my face, and called for the dog. She came, and we went over the fence in the side yard and down the hill to our neighbor.

As we neared, I could see them through the window. They were sitting down to dinner. Marcie came round and opened the door. I couldn't see Bill, but I was sure he was dialing the sheriff and loading up buckshot at the same time. This wasn't the first time they had taken me in.

That night I rode back to the house with the sheriff. Buck didn't answer the door, but I let the sheriff in. We found Buck passed out on the sofa, ESPN blaring. While the sheriff stood guard, I emptied my closet, taking the few items I owned, and the truck.

The remains of the pie were still sitting on the table when I left the house I had called home for twenty-two years.

The Proposal

"Let's eat in tonight," he said over breakfast, a twinkle in his eye.

I looked at him wondering what he had in mind. Would he propose tonight? There had been hints.

"I'll cook," he offered.

That was enough for me. "Ok but I won't be home till late, I've got a meeting."

His chin dropped down, his lips lost their smile.

"But, I'll be hungry," I said.

"Great." He smiled. "I think I'll barbecue."

"Sounds good."

When I returned that night, he had the grill glowing, and candles lit on the patio table. He handed me a glass of wine. He was wearing his "Kiss The Cook" apron. "Yum," I said. "Everything looks great, and I'm starving."

"Good, I'll put the steaks on, corn's done, and I'll get the salad," he said. As he walked away, I saw that he had on nothing but the apron. I smiled at that, he was making an impression.

I took a seat and noticed he used his mother's china. Perhaps this was the night. We'd been living together for a year and always talked about marriage one day.

He placed the steaks on the grill, and I heard them sizzle; he set the salad on the table. He had added avocado even though I knew he hated it. He was making this special for me. As he sat down to join me, a cannon roared, and the sounds of Boom Boom Boom pierced the night. I screamed in surprise; the sky was lit with a firework display to rival any Fourth of July celebration, but it wasn't even June.

Whether it was the sound of the canon or my cry, he jumped up suddenly. His knees knocked the glass-top table; his chair fell backward, and he reached for the umbrella in the table to steady himself. The umbrella swayed, he held tight, and together they tumbled to the ground. The wine glasses, the china, the glass-top table all shattered on the stone patio. I stood to help and caught sight of the grill; the steaks were engulfed in flames.

"Fire," I shouted as another volley of fireworks were launched.

"What?" he yelled over the din.

"Fire," I said. The fireworks floated down in the dark sky, the steaks flamed. He turned and scrambled out from under the umbrella. He bolted to the grill and in his haste, turned the propane up, not off. There was a sound like WHOOSH and flames shot up six feet as if to meet the descending fireworks.

"Damn," he said flapping his hands at his face.

On my way across the patio, I saw that the awning had caught fire and pointed yelling, "Fire."

He turned toward me, and I realized that whoosh burned off his eyebrows and the front part of his hair. I wanted to laugh, but glad he had the apron to protect himself.

"Fire," I screamed, and his eyes followed my point to the awning. I darted across the patio, grabbed the garden hose and turned it on. The nozzle was open, which is not usual, so as the pressure came up, it squirted him. Dripping wet, he sputtered, but I didn't pay attention, I aimed it at the awning, hoping it would not jump to the roof and yelled at him, "Call 9-1-1."

Ten minutes later the sounds of sirens filled the night, and I sat down, hose in hand. "Open the front door," I said. He was standing next to the grill looking down at his now drowned steaks.

"What?" he said.

"Go open the door. If you don't, they'll break it down."

The fire trucks were on our street, I heard their engines idle. I shouted out, "In the back yard."

At that moment, Fred, our next-door neighbor turned on his porch light and leaned over the fence. "What's going on?" he asked.

Before I could answer, the doorbell rang. I jumped up, ran into the house. It was bad enough having to replace the awning, the patio table and other things that had broken; I didn't want to add the front door to that. SPLAT. Two steps into the kitchen, I slipped and fell forward, slid across the floor, face first into the kitchen island. "What the ..." I shouted, and realized the kitchen window must have been open, and all the water I sprayed at the awning had also come in onto the kitchen floor. That's when I heard the sound of the hatchet coming through the front door.

What the fireman saw. A petite red-haired woman in a business suit lying on the kitchen floor, her nose broken and both eyes were blackening, the kitchen floor wet, and a smell of smoke. Outside glass glittered on the patio where the frame of a table with an umbrella still through its center lay on its side. A young man dripping wet, wearing only an apron appeared to be in shock, having lost his eyebrows, eyelashes and most of the hair above his forehead. He stood holding a BBQ fork over well-charred steaks. Water dripped from the remains of a blue and white-striped awning, and a quizzical neighbor chuckled, "Did she like the fireworks? Did she say yes?"

Blame It On Mercury

1.

Grace Steed was determined to put her life back on track. Tucked away in her mother's attic, she found proof of a lie which caused Grace to reconsider everything.

If asked, she would say that she chose the psychologist on equal parts of reputation and anonymity. Grace was someone known around town, she didn't want her troubles broadcast like dandelion seeds on a blustery day. Friends often recommended a local woman, Sydney Miller to those asking. Grace believed a woman would be better equipped to understand her dilemma.

She dressed in a dark blue pleated skirt, a navy sweater and wore a wide brimmed hat. When she arrived at the psychologist's office, the reception area was empty. After reading the posted sign, she realized it was a self-service waiting room. She pressed the button below the sign that read, "Press button to signal your arrival." She sat and waited. Grace was five minutes early, she prided herself on being punctual and prepared. Today she did not feel prepared at all. She reached inside her bag and tapped the manila envelope with her index finger, assuring herself the contents were real.

She chose the first chair, nearest the door. It was a high back Windsor upholstered in dark maroon leather with brass decorative tacks. There was an identical chair on her right with a small oak parsons table between. A table lamp with a brass base and linen shade stood on the table, brightly lit. Piled in front of it, in no particular order, was a collection of magazines that included *Sunset, Redbook, Field & Stream*, and *Coastal Living*. On the opposite wall was a frosted sliding glass window that might connect with a reception desk. On a small ledge, maybe four inches wide, was the displayed sign, "The Offices of Sydney P. Miller, Ph.D."

At the far end of the room, was a small settee where two people might sit. It was of the same maroon leather but the cushions seemed well worn. On the floor was a box of children's books which made her wonder if children had to sit in this austere room and occupy themselves while mummy and daddy had a session. Or worse yet, that the child had the session and mummy and siblings sat here and read books like "The Cat in the Hat" while sister or brother talked of inexplicable things.

The thought of those children caused Grace to tremble. She reached deep into her bag and removed the manila envelope. She held it in her hands and closed her eyes. She wondered again if she should take this step or let it be. *Can I undo the past? Should I?* She checked her watch, and returned the envelope to her bag.

Her watch displayed 9:59 a.m., she wondered if she would have to wait or if the session would start promptly? Grace picked up a magazine from the top of the stack and began to leaf through the glossy pages, working her way from the back of the book to the front. *What is the meaning of the way I read a magazine,* she wondered. She looked up, scrutinized the room. *Did the pressing of the button cause some video surveillance of the room? Perhaps opening the door triggered the video surveillance? Did I do anything I will regret? Did I blow into my hand and check my breath?* The self-questioning was about to undo her resolve.

I can still leave, she thought. *Once I am in the inner room, I'd be too embarrassed to leave.* She set the magazine down, stood up and reached for the entry door. At that moment the interior door opened and a young man stood there. He wore a white button down collar shirt, red bow tie, black slacks and polished shoes. He could not have been more than 30 years of age. She assumed he was a patient exiting his appointment and hesitated with her hand on the doorknob.

"Ms. Steed? Grace Steed?" he asked.

"Yes"

"Are you ready to begin?"

"Who are you?"

"I am Dr. Miller, Dr. Sydney Miller."

"But.... I thought Sydney was a woman..."

"I'm sorry. Were you referred to me?"

"Actually several women said...."

"Come in, let me explain."

They seemed at an impasse. Grace stood with her hand on the doorknob to exit the office, Sydney stood at the inner door waiting for Grace to make up her mind. Question marks hung in the air. Would Grace turn and start the session? Would Sydney be able to explain her appearance?

2.

Outside wind blew clouds across the valley shrouding the sun, and droplets of rain pelted the dusty windshields of cars. Mercury was in retrograde and the roosters crowed into the afternoon and the hens did not lay. Enough rain fell that the major intersection in tiny Cedar Meadows became clogged with slow vehicles, and the FedEx delivery van collided with Mrs. Perkins when she backed out of the post office on Crescent Street. She said that she had looked both ways, Stu Van der Wagon said that she had backed straight into the street at a higher than safe speed. When he applied the brakes, he slid on the oil-slick street and could not avoid the collision. An ambulance was called for Mrs. Perkins.

As the emergency vehicle sped down Fifth Avenue, Jim Jensen's pygmy goat galloped into its path. Luckily the driver was able to swerve and avoid hitting Pepper, the goat, but the ambulance clipped the side mirror off the mayor's new Chrysler. Bob Smith was at the wheel and he wasn't sure whether he should continue to the aid of Mrs. Perkins, or stop and report the accident to the mayor. His supervisor waved him to the scene of the accident at the post office.

The major's wife happened to be driving behind the ambulance and witnessed the mishap. She couldn't figure out why her husband's car was parked there on Fifth Avenue in the first place. He had told her he had business in the next town all day and not to expect him home till late. She parked her car and crossed the street to inspect the Chrysler; maybe it wasn't Hiz Honor's. On the dashboard was his "Mayor" nameplate, verifying that this was his car. She glanced up seeing Hiz Honor through the window of Mimi Grant's living room looking out at her. She shoved her hands on her hips and stared him down. *What in the world is he doing there?*

3.

Dr. Sydney P. Miller sat in a chair exactly like the chair in reception. Grace sat on the only other seat, a black micro-suede lounge opposite him. She thought it was a little stereotypical for a psychologist's office. *A couch, really?* There was a desk behind where the young man sat, and a low-lying table between them. It looked like a maple coffee table from the 1950's with a small spindle ledge around the corners of the table. On this table sat a single box of tissues.

Grace wanted to know why she had been told that Dr. Miller was a woman when she certainly looked like a man. She had heard from at least two people that they had at one time or another met with

Dr. Miller and had highly recommended her. *Clearly, this was not the correct Dr. Miller. Could this be her son? With the same name? Sydney was a non-specific gender name.*

"I thought you were a woman. In fact several people who referred me, said that they had met with a woman."

"I understand. I apologize for the confusion."

"Are you related to the other Dr. Sydney Miller?"

"I…uh…we're the same. I am a woman who is now living as a man."

Grace cleared her throat and stared at the flat front of the button down white oxford shirt. "You are…?"

"I…I have always felt out of place and after my own therapy sessions have embarked on this journey to right the error of my gender."

"Well...I never..." Grace didn't know what to say. *If I stand and leave I will worry about this all day and I won't be any closer to my own resolve.* "I think I've made a huge mistake."

"I'm sorry. Certainly if you are uncomfortable I will understand you leaving."

"No, not about you. About me!"

"What do you think is a mistake?" Sydney began the session.

4.

"Charlie," Mimi called from the bedroom. "I'm ready for my sentencing."

"Not now. Get dressed. We've got trouble." Charlie Browning barked. He stood at the window looking out. He wasn't sure what bothered him more; the fact that his brand new Chrysler had been sideswiped by the ambulance, or that Mrs. Browning had caught him in a lie.

"What the hell!" Mimi said walking into the living room. She was dressed in a black leather corset with a studded collar around her neck. She wobbled in the six-inch stilettoes. Charlie stood there still dressed in a black judge's robe, glaring out the window. She came across the room to see what he was scowling at. "Oh my," she said when she saw Charlie's wife staring in at them. She tried to cover her exposed body with her hands but quickly returned to the safety of the hallway and yelled, "What's going on here Charlie?"

Charlie was still locked in a stare with his wife of thirty-five years. She had been talking about renewing their marriage vows, she had hinted at a new wedding ring for the occasion. Instead he had bought the Chrysler claiming that as mayor he had a certain image to maintain. He knew this could be his undoing. *What can I possibly say that would renew her trust in me? How can I explain being here at Mimi's in the middle of the day?* He needed a plausible story.

Several years before, he had been caught with his pants down in the spare bedroom of a close friend's at a party. He had gotten off with the fabrication that someone had spilled a drink on his pants, and the hostess offered to quickly launder them, so no one would be the wiser. She had bought that one. Even if it meant letting the hostess put his new Perry Ellis wool gabardine slacks into the washing machine. But this was going to take a little more thought.

Eleanor Clark Browning looked down at the side mirror lying in the street. She bent over, picked it up, and gauged its weight.

Charlie Browning watched his wife pick up the mirror, then she did something extraordinary. She threw it across the lawn at the picture window in Mimi's front room. It struck the glass, and fell onto the floor barely five feet from where he stood.

The window shattered, dropping shards of glass on the floor. "What the hell," Mimi shouted at the sound of breaking glass. Charlie jumped back, alarmed, and watched Eleanor drive away.

5.

Corey Perkins stepped back from the tee on the third hole and frowned at his cell phone. He didn't like it when he was interrupted.

"Damn," he said reading the text. "Gotta' go." He dropped his club into the bag and hesitated. He wanted to take the cart back to the parking lot, but he had his partner's bag in the cart as well.

Sensing his hesitation, Walt Walters said, "I'll take you back to your car, and then come back and finish the round. Looks like I win by default, again."

"Don't remind me. Being the only doctor in town has its drawbacks."

"Tell me about it. Being the only lawyer in town. Anybody I know?"

"Actually, maybe you need to come along. Fender bender outside the post office. Ambulance on its way."

The phone rang then. "Let's go," he said to Walt. "Doc here," he said into the phone.

"Worse than I thought," he turned and said to Walt.

"What?"

"My mother! She's driving again and backed into the FedEx truck."

"She hurt?"

"Just shaken up. I hope."

"How old is she now?"

"Ninety-four next week. Can you imagine? She'll make it to one hundred if she'll quit driving. I thought I had her convinced. Well, now the car has to go."

6.

Susie Johnson made sure all the windows in her car were up, she turned up the volume on her radio. She hoped it would look like she was singing along with a song, but instead she was cussing out Velma and Brick Batterson. They had begged her to put their house on the market and sell it in a hurry, and for the past six weeks she had held open houses, posted flyers, and broadcast ads about the listing on the tricity area television station. Yesterday, a real estate agent from the neighboring town of Cedar Shores brought in a full price offer but Velma decided that maybe now wasn't the best time to sell. She sat with Velma and Brick and reminded them that it was their idea to sell.

"Worst case scenario? You owe that Cedar Shores agent and me the commission even if you don't sell. Read the agreement."

"But I'm not sure that I want to move. We've lived here so long."

"Velma, when you called and said you wanted to list, you said Brick wasn't able to keep up with the yard work, that you had problems with the stairs, and you wanted to move into the senior apartments downtown. In fact, you said that Lacey was keeping number eight open for you."

"I know. I know I said all that and at the time I was thinking it was all true, but..."

"But what?"

"Suddenly when I got up this morning everything seemed different. You know different?"

"What's so different? You still have ten acres, the tractor is broken and Brick can't get around. What's different?"

"Sally Sue said Mercury's in retrograde and while it is, don't make any big decisions. Things go wonky when Mercury is out of sync."

"For gosh sakes Velma. When does Sally Sue say we can make decisions again? Can I tell the buyers that if they wait a week, you'll be able to review their offer then?"

"Well, I dunno..."

"Brick, you need to pay attention. You can't let Velma ruin this chance for you to unburden yourself from this property. It's a good offer. It's full price!"

She couldn't persuade them either way. She'd have to say that she presented the offer and due to extenuating circumstances they are unable to respond to the offer at this time. What she wanted to say is that they are crazy people, but that was unprofessional. *Mercury in retrograde, what was that?*

7.

Grace Steed heard the ambulance, even from the inside office of Dr. Sydney P. Miller, Ph.D. She wondered who might need medical attention.

"What is the nature of this mistake?" Dr. Miller asked.

Grace shifted in her seat. She scooted forward, then back, slouched, sat erect as if there were bugs crawling beneath her. She stood, shaking the folds of her skirt and then sat down again.

"Is everything alright?" Dr. Miller asked. To the eye, Ms. Steed seemed a solidly built woman with a no-nonsense attitude. She wasn't very tall, but she had a powerful build. She had shock white hair that she kept cut short and a kindly round face with doe-brown eyes. Dr. Miller tried to place her, she seemed familiar, and he knew her name from the local paper. He couldn't decide if it was from the society page or the local political scene.

"Oh I'm just fidgeting. This goes back a long way and recently I discovered something that makes it all come back. I wish I would have fought harder."

"Is this what you wanted to talk to me about?"

"It is. I've never talked to anyone about this."

"What is the beginning? Let's start there."

"When I was fifteen I thought I was madly in love. My parents weren't pleased about it and forbade me from seeing him. I was pregnant."

"How did they react to that?"

"They were horrified. They said for me and my reputation, but my mother seemed more concerned that I hadn't had a coming out party. Then she'd look down at my belly and say, 'now you're coming out, aren't you?' They sent me to live with someone they said was a relative who lived far away on a farm. She made me work for her and had little sympathy for me or my condition."

"It must have been hard. What about the boyfriend?"

"I wrote to him. He professed his love but then he stopped writing. When I came home, he was nowhere to be found. I never heard from him again, nor did anyone else I knew. He vanished."

"And the baby?"

Grace reached across the table for a tissue and blew her nose. She took another tissue and crumpled it in her right fist. "I was told that the baby died during birth. I was told that this often happens with teen pregnancy, the mother's body isn't mature enough to nourish the baby. I was heart broken. They wouldn't let me see the baby. They wouldn't let me have a funeral. They said that a priest was there at the hospital and sent the baby to heaven." She wiped her eyes.

"Boy or girl?"

Grace looked at Dr. Miller. The irony of the question made her smile, breaking the tension. *I guess I could ask you the same question* she thought. "They wouldn't tell me. I searched and searched but can find no records of my stay at that hospital. Is that allowed? Can they erase my baby from their records?"

"When was this?"

"It was forty years ago." Grace dabbed her eyes and blew her nose again. "This is so unlike me to be emotional, but..."

"Did something happen recently?"

"My mother died. She had been ailing for several years and while our relationship never mended after the pregnancy, we were always civil. When she died, everything came to me as the only child. I went to clean out the house. I was going to sell it, In the attic I found a trunk that was filled with grammar school papers. At first I thought they were mine, but then the dates, the material on them, made me realize they were not mine. The photographs were of a boy from infancy to pre-teen. Why would my mother have all this? Who was he? I scrutinized everything in that trunk.

I now believe that my baby didn't die in birth. I believe that they took the baby and put him in someone's care and for many years, there was communication between my mother and my son. She never told me. I never knew. I was robbed. My son was robbed of a mother who would have loved him."

8.

After Charlie left, Mimi called the hardware store and asked them to send someone out to replace the window. She knew Henry would come and then he would have all kinds of questions about how the window got broken. She picked up the mirror from the mayor's car, and wondered why he hadn't taken it with him. She stuffed it behind a pillow on the sofa, went back to the bedroom to clean up and put things right. Henry would be sniffing around trying to figure out who she was keeping company with. Hard to live in a small town and have to encounter your ex-husband every time you needed some hardware.

When Henry arrived, she greeted him and he embraced her; she could smell the cheap cologne. He was here for more than the window.

9.

Mrs. Patty Perkins was sitting on the bed in the Emergency Care Facility. She was hooked up to an IV drip, a heart monitor, a blood pressure monitor, and had a thermometer stuck under her tongue. Corey checked the chart and looked at an x-ray then came bedside.

"Mom, how are you feeling?"

"Good. Seems all kinda' silly. I just got rear ended by that crazy Stuart Van der Wagon. Always was a punk racecar driver. How are you son?"

"I'm fine. For someone who only got to play two holes on his day off."

"What day is it?"

"I was going to ask you."

"Well, it's your birthday isn't it?"

"It is. Now let's make sure you're in good enough condition to go to dinner with me tonight."

"Tell me something you want for your birthday."

"I want your car keys."

"But you have a nice car. Why do you want mine?"

10.

"What else did you find?" Dr. Miller asked.

"There are elementary school papers and letters that he wrote to his grandmother. Those papers have a name on them. The boy is named Jasper P. That's all that's on the papers. There is no birth certificate, no adoption papers."

"Have you been through all your mother's papers?"

"I have. I've cleaned out the safety deposit box at the bank, and met with her lawyer. I confronted him about this. He said he had no knowledge, he started representing my mother about ten years ago. All the legal documents had listed me as the only next of kin, the only heir."

"And your mother never mentioned any of this?"

"Never."

"Nor your father?"

"No. I thought we were close, my father and I. But after I came back from having the baby, we were never that close again. I took that as his disappointment in me."

"What do you want to happen?"

"I'm not sure. I have this name and the date of birth. That's all. I don't know where to go from here. There were no envelopes with all the items in the trunk. I've gone through my mother's address books and found nothing other than the people I already know."

"Is it possible that your parents arranged for this child to go to someone they knew? Who had been your parents' lawyer then? Was it possible that a priest or minister handled this? What church did they attend?"

"I've not thought about that. I was thinking of going online. There are online sites for reuniting parents with children that were adopted. I'm not sure if that is what I should do or not."

"What makes you hold back?"

"Fear. Fear of not finding him. Fear of being rejected. After all, forty years have gone by. He's an adult. He probably has his own family. I would just be intruding, wouldn't I?"

"You don't know. Perhaps he knows that he was adopted and always wondered about his birth parents."

"But what if he has never known. It would be horrible to find out now, wouldn't it? Do I have the right to interrupt his life? Now that I know this, I don't think I can go back to how I was before."

11.

Walt Walters arrived at his office just after eleven with a steaming cup of espresso in one hand. He didn't have any appointments on his calendar and was looking forward to a quiet day. The phone was ringing as he unlocked the door. His office was next door to the courthouse, one of the oldest buildings in Cedar Meadows, located downtown across from the post office. He set the coffee down and picked up the phone only to hear a click on the other end. He removed his suit jacket and hung it in the closet. It was important for him to look professional. He was the only lawyer in town and had business at the courthouse nearly every day.

When the phone rang again, it was a call from the mayor's wife.

"Walt, it's me, Eleanor, Eleanor Clark Browning."

"Yes, Mrs. Browning, how may I help you?"

"I'd like to come see you today. I have something very important to discuss."

"Did you have a particular time in mind? I've got some time open this afternoon."

"How about two?"

"That's fine. I'll see you then."

As he hung up he wondered what that was about. He knew the Clark family had their own lawyer over in Mt. Hastings. *It probably isn't anything important.*

He took a pencil and wrote her name in between two and three on the calendar. The phone rang again.

"Walters Law Office," he said.

"Walt, this is Grace Steed. I need your help. Could we meet today?"

"Grace, it's nice to hear from you. I have an opening at three. Will that work for you?"

"Why yes. Perfect. Thank you Walt, I'll see you then."

Interesting, thought Walt. Grace Steed had been his fifth grade teacher. She usually came to see him when she was raising funds for the PTA or some other school cause. This didn't sound like one of those calls, this sounded like she may need some legal advice.

Well, it looks like I'm going to have a busy afternoon, so I'd better catch up on my correspondence right away. Walt opened the top left desk drawer and removed a stack of files. He turned on the green-shaded bankers lamp and switched on the computer. He pulled the keyboard in front of him and began typing. He had a secretary who typed up his legal briefs and did some research, but she only worked two afternoons a week. He did most of his own correspondence.

The next call came about an hour later from Stu Van der Wagon. Apparently he was the one in the Fed Ex truck that Mrs. Perkins had backed into. He wanted to be sure that he was not going be sued by the Perkins family. Walt suggested that he call his insurer and get back to him only if there was a problem. Stu Van der Wagon was Walt's brother-in-law, married to his sister Lisa. There was no billing of family members.

"Look Walt, I know that you and Mrs. Perkin's son are close, but that lady must be a hundred years old and she shouldn't be driving."

"Stu, if she backed into you, you are in the clear. Why are you so worried about this?"

"I'm a professional driver. I need the job. If they think I am not doing a good job, they'll can me."

"Okay, calm down. I was with Corey when he got the call. He followed up with his mom and she's fine. I heard there are witnesses and believe me, Corey is taking the car from her."

12.

At five minutes before two o'clock, Walt put on his jacket, straightened his tie, and cleared his desk. He took a new legal pad from the supply cabinet. Right at two, there was a knock on the door, and Walt opened the door to Eleanor Clark Browning.

Eleanor was from one of the founding families of Cedar Meadows. Her father had run the local mercantile store, which later became a grocery and department store. He sold off his businesses and most of his real estate holdings in Cedar Meadows' heyday.

That set his family up as the most well to do family in town. Eleanor was a smart woman who had attended Vassar, and had travelled throughout Europe before settling down and marrying Charlie Browning. Charlie had been the postmaster for the county after returning from Vietnam a decorated marine. He ran a successful campaign for mayor and had held that post now for nearly twenty years.

Eleanor was dressed in a pale yellow linen suit. Her hair and makeup were always picture perfect. She smiled at Walt and shook hands with him, then seemed at a loss. Walt gestured toward one of the two chairs facing his desk. She nodded and took one, laying her purse on the seat of the other.

"What can I help you with today Mrs. Browning."

"Oh, call me Eleanor."

"Eleanor," he said.

"Well, I've had it. I want a divorce."

"On what grounds? In this state we need to have some proven grounds in order to file for divorce. We do have some very good counselors to try and help mediate. Often these misunderstandings…"

"No mediators, no counselors. I want a divorce on the grounds of spousal abuse, philandering, infidelity."

"That's pretty strong language. Do you have proof?"

"Proof? I saw him with my own eyes. And this isn't the first time. There have been dozens of times that things didn't add up, but this time, I caught him in the act."

"In the act? I'm sorry to hear that. Who is the other party?"

"Mimi Grant!"

"Have you talked with your husband about this? Is he willing to grant you a divorce without going through the courts? If he is, then we can keep it all very quiet."

"No. It just happened this morning. I was coming from the beauty parlor when I saw the ambulance hit the mayor's car. I wasn't even sure it was his car because he told me he would be out of town all day, and not to expect him till late tonight. But it was his car. I looked up at Mimi's house, and he was standing in the front room looking out. Mimi came strutting out in her all together. He said something to her, and she went away. But he didn't come out and talk to me. I think he was wearing something other than the suit he had on when he left this morning too."

"The first step would be for you to retain my services. I can draw up the documents and serve him. We can probably accomplish this within the next day or two. Will you be staying at your home?"

"Takes that long? I was hoping we could do it today and be done with it."

"If you prefer not to talk with him, I can make a phone call and have him come in and see me and let him know your intention..."

"Fine. I want to retain your services and let's get this paperwork going. What else do you need to know?"

"Do you have any special sort of agreement regarding finances?"

"Do you mean can he access my family money?"

"Yes, that would be a start."

"No, Daddy kept it in a trust that only I can access. He knew Charlie wasn't all that trustworthy. War hero, so what."

"I've got a long list of questions to go over with you. Let's get started, but I have to let you know that I have another appointment this afternoon at three."

13.

Walt exited Eleanor and assured her he would have the papers ready for her signature at nine the following morning. She told him she would stay at the family home in Cedar Shores that night and not to let Charlie know where she was. As he opened the door for Eleanor to leave, he found Grace Steed standing there.

"Come in Grace," he said.

"Walt, thank you for seeing me today. It's been quite a day for me."

"What's going on?"

"I need to be sure that we have that client confidentiality thing going on here."

"We do."

"You are the second person I have told this to and the second person I have told today. The other was a psychologist."

"Go on."

"When I was fifteen, I became pregnant and went to a hospital to have the baby. Afterwards, they told me the baby hadn't made it. They said that a priest had sent the baby to heaven. I wasn't allowed to see the baby. I contacted the hospital recently, there is no record of my ever having been there. No record of the birth of the baby. Nothing."

"Was it local here?"

"No, it was just outside of Akron, Ohio. My parents sent me to live with a relative until the baby came. They are long dead and there are no other relatives in that area. Maybe they weren't even relatives because I knew nothing of them until I was sent to live with them."

"Grace, I had no idea. How can I help?"

"When mother died, I cleared out her house. Up in the attic I found a trunk filled with pictures of a boy. There are also pictures he drew and letters he wrote to my parents calling them grandmother and grandfather. There are a couple of school worksheets that he wrote his name on. That is the only clue I have as to who he is. The name printed was "Jasper P."

"When was this? How old would he be?"

"If it is my son, he would be forty." She laid the manila envelope on the desk before her.

"Are there any clues in the photos about where he was raised? Any other people in the photos? The name of the school? Anything else?" Walt opened the envelope and scanned the contents.

"I found that about a month ago. I was shocked. I didn't know what to do. I called the hospital in Akron. When I didn't get anywhere, I went there and waited for them to pull records from that time. There was no record of the birth or my stay. Somehow my parents did this so that I would never find him."

14.

The mayor drove his Chrysler over to Cedar Motors and asked that they replace the mirror as quickly as possible. Harold, the service manager said he'd have to order the part, "The model being the newest one and all." Somewhat perplexed by this, the mayor headed to his office. He was still trying to concoct the perfect story for his wife.

First he thought if he could replace the mirror, he could claim it hadn't been his car that Eleanor saw on the street. Not succeeding with that, he was thinking about having someone else drive the car. *Maybe I should have asked Harold to give it a spin and take the blame. Maybe I could have Harold call the house and claim that while he was checking the car out the accident had occurred. Maybe Eleanor didn't really see me inside Mimi's house. But why did she throw the mirror through the window if not to throw it at me?*

When he reached city hall, he found his parking spot occupied by the sheriff's car. Now he would have to drive half way round the block and park at the courthouse and walk back. On his walk back, he saw Eleanor come out of Walt Walters' office. *What the hell is she doing there?* He watched her walk in her purposeful way. He knew clearly now that she had indeed seen him at Mimi's and she was up on her high horse. He was in real trouble.

He slunk along the sidewalk keeping in the shadows so she wouldn't see him. As he passed the Blitz Jewelry Store he had a brilliant idea. *I'll buy that ring that Eleanor wants and surprise her tonight. I'll say that's why she saw me at Mimi's to pick it up. Everyone knows Mimi doesn't keep regular hours at the store.* He felt a plan coming together.

He jaywalked across the street and went into his office to see if there was any pressing mayoral business before calling Mimi. When he opened the door to the reception area in the city hall he was overcome by a cacophony of sounds. Jim Jensen was there with his pygmy goat and Stu Van der Wagon was yelling at him. The sheriff was in the midst of this trying to calm down the parties. On the outskirts stood three teenagers who were covered head to toe in bright florescent paint: pink, orange, green, yellow. It was everywhere, on their faces, in their hair and totally covering their clothing. Two of their mothers were standing nearby hemming and hawing over the mess. Miss Elsie, the long time city clerk was standing on her desk blowing a whistle trying to get everyone's attention. Charlie could hear her yelling, "One at a time! One at a time!" No one wanted to give up their debate, each continued and raised their voices to counter the others.

Charlie looked from one face to another, then quietly walked around them and went into his office and closed the door. On his made-to-order oak swivel chair with authentic leather seat was a chicken. A Rhode Island Red hen to be exact, and on the floor was a broken egg. "Hells Bells," Charlie said. He opened his bottom desk drawer and withdrew the bottle of Johnny Walker Red. Without any further distractions, he unscrewed the cap and took a long swallow from the bottle. *This has not been my day.*

The door burst open and Elsie came in followed by Jim Jenson, his pygmy goat, Stu Van der Wagon, and the sheriff. Before he could return the bottle to its place, the hen rattled her wings and lifted off landing on the back of the goat, which bucked striking the sheriff. In his bewilderment about who struck him, he pulled his pistol and fired. The first bullet went into the ceiling tile, the next through the window overlooking the courthouse garden. The third bullet embedded itself in the mayor's face in his prized photo of Hiz Honor with the then governor who went on to become president of the United States. At the sound of the weapon being discharged, all fell silent. The hen clucked softly and walked through the doorway.

It took several minutes before everyone realized that no one had been shot. The mayor instructed the sheriff to arrest anyone who spoke in the next ten minutes. He then asked the sheriff to explain what the problem was. Stu started to say something but the mayor pointed his finger at him and he stopped mid word. The sheriff explained about the goat causing the ambulance to sideswipe the mayor's car.

The mayor, thinking quickly, asked if anyone knew who had left the mayor's car there. He said that it had been missing for several hours this morning and when it was returned, the side mirror was broken off. Everyone looked from one to the other and shrugged their shoulders. No one had any idea who, other than the mayor, would have been driving the mayor's new Chrysler.

"I want to file a stolen car report," the mayor said to the sheriff.

"Is it still missing?"

"Well, no."

"Then..."

"I want to file a report. I want it investigated. My car has been damaged."

"I'll get right on it."

"And I want an accident report filed for the damage..."

"Well, this here goat..." began the sheriff.

"That's my goat and she just wandered," said Jim Jensen.

The mayor looked at Jim Jensen and pointed his finger. Jim closed his mouth and stepped back.

"Who was driving the ambulance?" the mayor asked.

"Why that was Bob Smith," said Stu.

The mayor turned quickly and pointed his finger at Stu. Stu stepped back.

"Was there anything else missing from the car?" the sheriff asked.

"Why, yes," said the mayor. "I purchased a diamond ring for Mrs. Browning. I left it in the glove compartment, and it's not there now. It's a very expensive ring."

The sheriff began writing this down.

"Elsie, do you think you can clean up this broken egg. What was the chicken doing in my office?"

"It's been a crazy day," said the sheriff. "Did you see those kids out there? They got into a paint fight. Filled water balloons with paint and pelted them at one another."

"Messy, but harmless," said the mayor.

"Only they did it in the yard behind the commercial cleaners. They ruined all the sheets hanging on the clotheslines," reported the sheriff.

"Well it sounds like things have quieted down now. You can finish up this business in your office. Let me know when the stolen car report is ready." He waved them out of his office. He closed the door. Finding the bottle of Johnny Walker Red still in his hand, he uncapped it and took another long swallow.

Then he called Mimi and arranged for her to meet him at the jewelry store. He'd need that receipt for the insurance claim.

15.

Henry hitched up his trousers and refastened his suspenders. He stood back and admired the new window there in Mimi's parlor. Mimi called from the kitchen, "Cup of coffee before you go?"

"You bet! Thanks Honey," he said. *Maybe I shouldn't have said Honey* he thought, *but the way things turned out this afternoon, why not?*

The phone rang and he heard Mimi answer. He wondered who was calling her. He really wanted to know if she was seeing anyone. Maybe this time they could work out their differences and get back together. Henry didn't understand what went wrong in the first place. He had always been in love with Mimi.

"Hold on, I got company," he heard her say.

"Oh, okay. I'll be there in fifteen," said Mimi.

"Got a problem?" Henry asked.

"No, got a customer who wants me to go open up the Blitz for him."

"Oh, who thinks they're such big stuff for that? The mayor?"

"Yeah, it is the mayor." She looked at Henry. *What does he know?* "Wants me to open the jewelry store just so he can buy his wife some fancy ring."

"Well, I guess he's got the money to buy it, what with that fancy new car of his."

Henry sipped his coffee, savoring his time alone with Mimi. He wondered if he had the money to buy her a fancy ring, if that would bring her back to him.

16.

Walt arrived at the restaurant at a quarter past six. He asked the maître d' if the bottles of wine he had ordered had been opened and were ready to serve. He was assured that all was as he requested and ushered him into the private banquet room. Tonight was his best friend's birthday and despite all the craziness of the day, he was going to make it a special night. He had invited several friends and had preselected a menu for the evening. With Corey and his mother, there would be twelve for dinner. Of course, Corey's wife, Barbara and their twin daughters would be there. He had invited Olivia Newsome, the new high school math teacher. He had taken her out on a first date and was looking forward to having her meet his closest friends tonight. She would be coming with Vern and Susie Johnson; Vern was the principal at the high school and Susie was the real estate agent for Cedar Meadows.

By six-thirty everyone had arrived. Walt asked everyone to raise a glass in a toast to Corey.

"My friends, let's raise our glass to the best doctor in all of Cedar Meadows."

"Here, here"

"Happy Birthday Corey."

"Happy Birthday!"

"Wait! I want to say something," said Patty Perkins. "She pulled herself to her full height of five feet and raised her glass. "To my sweet, sweet son. I remember everything in all these forty years. Despite what you call yourself, you'll always be Jasper

Cornelius Perkins to me. Named after my father and my late husband. Happy Birthday son."

"Jasper?"

"Cornelius?"

"Oh Corey, you are in for it now," his wife said.

Olivia was sitting on Walt's right and she asked him a question. He didn't hear her because he was laughing along with everyone else at the name of his best friend. He didn't know him by anything other than Corey, or occasionally Doc.

"What'd you say?"

"I said what a nice party," Olivia said.

"Yes," he said, "and wait till you taste the food."

"Ask him what I gave him for his birthday today," Patty Perkins said to her granddaughters.

"What?" the twins chimed together. "Dad, what did Grammy give you?"

"Oh," he said, "She gave me her car."

"Why?" they asked. *What did dad want with Grammy's old clunker?*

Dinner was served: a cup of clam chowder, followed by a Caesar salad, then a bacon-wrapped filet mignon, potatoes Romanoff, fresh asparagus, and baked Alaska for dessert. The conversation and the wine flowed freely.

"What the heck was going on today?"

"The sheriff was run ragged."

"Did you hear about the ruckus in the mayor's office?"

"You mean about his car getting hit by the ambulance?"

"His new Chrysler?"

"It was stolen I heard."

"There was a big paint disaster over on Third Street."

"Mercury in retrograde."

"What?" Walt leaned in close to Olivia. "What did you say?"

"I said Mercury is in retrograde. When it turns out of its orbit away from us, tides change, our gravity is lessened, all things can go haywire."

"Really?"

"Is that what is going on?"

"My clients told me that," Susie Johnson chimed in. "They are usually very quiet and responsible people but today they were coming from left field. I brought them a full price offer, and they didn't bat an eye but said with Mercury in retrograde they shouldn't make any important decisions."

"Never heard of it."

"Me either."

"How long does it last?"

"Usually just a couple of days, then everything returns to normal. But…"

"Thank God!"

"Wait, but what?"

"But we've got the triple whammy – not only is Mercury in retrograde, but we have a full moon, and it landed on Friday the thirteenth," Olivia said.

"You've got to be kidding me!"

17.

At seven, the mayor became concerned that Eleanor had not returned home. He poured himself a cocktail when he came home and left the jewelry store receipt out for Eleanor to see. He would claim that he bought the ring and left it in the car, the car had been stolen but before he could report it missing, it had been returned with the mirror broken off and the ring missing. If there was any doubt in her mind, that should be enough to push her over the edge to believing him. At the florist, he picked up a dozen yellow roses and put them in a vase on the dining room table. *Where was she?*

Of course, he still had the ring, but that was another matter for later, if she didn't buy the first story.

By seven-thirty the Mayor had several cocktails and when he stopped to consider it, he hadn't eaten anything since he had a bowl of Raisin Bran at seven that morning.

He rummaged around and found Eleanor's address book and began to consider who he should call. *If she were mad at him who would she confide in? Who would she go and stay with? Would she check into a hotel? Would she... Yes! She would go to the family home on the lake in Cedar Shores.*

He went to her closet and looked to see if she had packed a bag. He really couldn't tell. He stood scratching his head. He didn't have a clue what to look for. Her closet seemed full but he didn't know enough about women's clothing or fashion to know if anything was missing. He stood peering into the closet.

18.

Walt drove Olivia home. He was extra careful because he drank a bit more than usual. Thinking about it, he added, *what with Mercury in retrograde, and* chuckled softly.

"What's funny?" Olivia asked.

"Oh I was just thinking about all the crazy things that happened today. Usually it's pretty boring here in Cedar Meadows. That scene they described in the mayor's office today, that was pretty unusual. And all this Mercury in retrograde stuff."

"Yes, most people don't take astrology seriously."

"You do?"

"I do. I majored in astronomy and there are a lot of things we know nothing about. We think man is the center of the universe, but we are insignificant."

"Astronomy. Astrology. I thought they were totally different."

"They are different. Astronomy is the science that includes everything outside the earth's atmosphere, the stars, and the planets. Astrology is a belief that the positioning of the stars and planets affect the way events occur on earth."

"Well, I guess I better pay closer attention." He smiled at her.

She smiled back. "Funny how no one seemed to know Corey's real name. How long have you known him?"

"Gee, Corey and I go back to grade school sometime. I remember we were in Boy Scouts and went on a lot of hikes and camping trips. Sometime around then is when we became best friends."

"That's a long time."

"It is. I don't recall him ever being called Jasper..."

Walt began to consider. *Mrs. Perkins is ninety-four; Corey is forty making her fifty-four when he was born.* "That's pretty old to have a baby, isn't it?"

"What is?" Olivia asked.

"Fifty-four?"

"Yeah! Up until they started fertility treatments, it was pretty much unheard of? Why do you ask?"

She wondered, Does he think I am fifty-four? Does he think I am too old to start a family? Does he want a family? Why is he still single at forty?

"I was just thinking out loud. Sorry."

"No really, why did you bring it up?"

"Client came to see me today. It has to do with what we talked about. I can't be more specific."

19.

Charlie picked up the phone and called Eleanor's cell phone. He knew it wouldn't work at the lake house, but maybe she wasn't there. It rang three times, then he heard her message.

"El, it's me. Where are you?"

He hung up. He looked at his watch and thought he would call her again in about a half hour. He poured himself another drink.

20.

Eleanor sat in the back row of the movie theatre in Cedar Shores. She had gone to the lake house but found it cold and uninviting. She had opted to go and see a comedy hoping it might lift her spirits. She felt her cell phone vibrate and she looked at the caller id. It was a call from home; Charlie must be looking for her. She smiled.

After meeting with Walt, she had gone home to pack a bag. The sheriff phoned, he was looking for Charlie, but thought it okay to tell her.

"Let him know I've got the stolen vehicle report for him to sign. And Eleanor, I'm really sorry about them stealing your ring."

"My ring?"

"Oh shit! Sorry. I guess I wasn't supposed to say anything about that. The mayor said that he bought it as a gift for you, and it was stolen out of his car today. Forget I said it okay, in case it was supposed to be a surprise."

Oh it is a surprise all right, she thought.

21.

At eight-fifteen, Charlie picked up the phone and dialed Eleanor again. It rang three times then, went to voicemail.

"El, it's me Charlie," he said. Realizing he was slurring his s's he tried to slow his speech down. "Babe, I'm really getting worried. Please call."

He poured another drink. The Johnny Walker bottle was empty. He went into the kitchen to see if there was another one. He noticed the calendar that Eleanor kept on the desk in the kitchen. He looked at the date and saw that she had written "35th Anniversary."

I had forgotten it was today. No wonder she was mad.

22.

Olivia lived in the apartment building downtown. It was a short drive from the restaurant. Walt walked her to her door and thanked her for a pleasant evening.

"I'd like an opportunity to show you around outside of downtown," he said.

"I'd like that," she said.

He leaned in to steal a kiss, she turned her head, and his lips landed on her cheek. Not sure what that meant, he decided against making another attempt. He stepped back, smiled, got in the car and headed home.

Coming back through the downtown, he saw the mayor driving his Chrysler. He waved. The mayor swerved and careened into the fire hydrant shearing it off its base. A plume of water rose filling the engine compartment.

Yikes, that's going to ruin his car for sure, Walt thought.

Seeing the mayor struggle, he stopped the car and went to help him out of the Chrysler. Upon opening the door, Walt was struck by a whiskey fog that seemed to surround the mayor.

"Let me help you out," Walt said.

"I can get out on my own thank you," said Charlie.

"Mayor, I think we need to call for help."

"Why am I in the lake?" he said, reacting to the water that was spewing over the car. "What the hell's going on here? Whose in charge?"

Walt reached in and grabbed the mayor by his upper arm and tried to drag him from the car. The mayor was wearing his suit jacket, but no pants. He was in his boxer shorts, and had only socks on his feet.

"Sir, where are you going?" Walt asked.

"I have a date with my wife. I'm late. I can't be late. Let me go." He wrenched himself away from Walt and fell back across the front seat of the car. Water continued to stream from the broken hydrant.

Walt shrugged and pulled his phone from his pocket and dialed.

"What is the nature of your emergency?" asked the operator.

"This is Walt Walters in Cedar Meadows. A fire hydrant has been sheared off, and we need some assistance. Yes, please send an ambulance as well."

"Sir, help is on its way."

"I said I don't need any help. Who the hell left the sprinklers on?"

"Your honor, you struck the hydrant."

"I did no such thing. I'm late for my anniversary. Please get out of my way."

"Sir, have you spoken with your wife this afternoon."

"Who?"

"Your wife?"

"Of course, I have a wife. Now I must be on my way."

"Here comes the sheriff."

"Why did you call him? He's an idiot. He had a goat in my office today. And a chicken."

The sheriff pulled up and turned off the water at the main. The ambulance arrived, and Walt backed away from the scene. He was wet and getting cold. "Mercury in retrograde," he muttered as he drove home. *Can't return to normal fast enough for me.*

23.

The wind blew at fifty miles an hour most of the night making it difficult for utility workers to sleep. They were called out to repair the broken fire hydrant, then to clear felled trees, and restring power lines. Citizens who slept missed all the excitement. Those awakened by the wind found that they had no water or electricity. It was a long, dark night.

As dawn broke, the wind retreated, the sun rose to a clear and crisp day; the sky was cloudless.

Children woke in a good mood, roosters crowed, hens were laying.

The commercial cleaners on Third Street found that the neon paint was water-based and washed easily out of their laundry. The three teenage boys showered and found that all traces of color were gone, somewhat to their chagrin.

Jim Jensen's goat stayed in her pen, happily munching on dandelions and an old tuna fish can.

Stu Van der Wagon loaded his Fed Ex truck with packages to deliver noting that the delivery to him had been on time and in good order.

Eleanor Clark Browning locked up the lake house and headed back to town. She had an appointment with Walt Walters at nine and didn't want to be late. As she reached the town limits, her cell phone came back to life. She had three voicemails. The first two were from Charlie worried about her. *Sweet,* she thought, *but you are a scoundrel.* The third message was from Doc Perkins. Charlie had been in an accident and was being taken to the Mt. Hastings Hospital. That message had been left after ten the night before. *That was nearly twelve hours ago.* She hung a U-turn and headed to Mt. Hastings.

24.

Walt Walters sat in his office going through old records. He wasn't sure what to do with the information he had uncovered. It appeared to him that the mystery of what happened to Grace's child was not so well hidden. He wished he could talk with Corey about it. He realized he wasn't exactly within the confines of his jurisdiction. He had to puzzle out how to pass on what he knew.

25.

Mimi woke to an awful noise. As she brushed the sleep from the corners of her mind, she sorted out that the noise was coming from her bedroom, not from outside. She couldn't fathom what it was. *It's almost as bad as Henry snoring,* she thought. Then she looked and it was Henry, snoring right beside her, in her bed. *Good Lord what have I done?*

"Morning sweets. Have another go?" Henry said with a twinkle in his eye.

26.

Grace Steed had only one appointment on her calendar today. She was having lunch with Patty Perkins. She and Patty had worked together on several school board issues over the years and Patty had suggested that they get together and talk about the calendar for the upcoming year. Grace was still feeling disoriented from her meetings the day before. She had kept all this to herself for so long and now to have let it out, it felt overwhelming. She felt vulnerable, open to pain and hurt. *It would be easy to call and beg off the meeting today. I could truthfully say I am feeling out of sorts. Better to get on with life and get refocused than keep on this other path.*

27.

Walt Walters noted the time at half past nine, Mrs. Browning had been due at nine. The divorce papers were filled out and ready for her signature. It was not unusual for a person to change their mind, especially when they had been married as long as the Brownings. He placed the papers into a manila folder and carefully filed it away. He wondered how the mayor was after last night. He called Corey to find out.

"Corey, it's Walt."

"Morning. What's up?"

"Did you get much sleep last night?"

"Oh not bad. I rode up to Mt. Hastings with the mayor then left him in their hands."

"How is he?"

"Best I know he should be fine. I think he was drunk, that's all. But never assume. Hey thanks for the great party last night."

"You bet. Is that really your name? Jasper Cornelius?"

"Yeah! I had it legally changed to Corey when I was in med school. Mom doesn't know that, but if I wasn't going to use the name, why have it and have to explain it. I didn't want to be one of those J dot somebodies."

"Hey, don't I know that, Walter Walters. I've always wondered if my parents were drunk when they named me or just lacked imagination. I was going to ask you about something. Do you have a second?"

"Sure, what's up?"

"Do you have any experience with adoption?"

"Why you thinking of adopting? Adopting a wife maybe?"

"No. Ha Ha! I have a client and was just looking for some advice."

"Sorry got my daughters the old fashioned way."

"Well have a great day. We'll have to reschedule golf."

"Next day off looks like Sunday."

"Sounds good to me."

28.

Eleanor arrived at Mt. Hastings Hospital and left her car at the emergency door. She hurried in asking for information on the mayor. No one she encountered recognized her or knew anything about the mayor. She was directed to the nurses' station.

"Whom are you asking for?"

"My husband."

"His name?"

"Oh dear me. Yes, of course. Charlie Browning, he's the mayor in Cedar Meadows."

"Mr. Browning was brought into emergency last night. Hmm. He was admitted early this morning and had some tests. It looks like he is due to be discharged later this morning. He is in room 4-B. You go to your left, take the elevator to the fourth floor and then go to ward B."

"Thank you. Thank you very much."

In the elevator, Eleanor realized she is relieved that he is alive so she can divorce him. The irony was not lost on her and she began to giggle. As the doors opened, she was doubled over, laughing hysterically. Unable to regain her composure, two attendants came to her side and asked if she was all right.

"Yes, fine. I'm fine." She giggled. "Where is ward B?"

29.

Grace entered the restaurant a few minutes before noon. She was to meet Patty Perkins at twelve.

"Grace Steed, you are looking fit. How good of you to meet me here," said Patty.

"Mrs. Perkins, you are as well." Grace sat across the table.

"Grace, you can call me Patty, everyone does. We've known each other long enough for that."

"Yes of course. But I do feel more comfortable calling you Mrs. Perkins."

"Why do you suppose that is?"

"When I first met you, you were the principal at the high school and I was a student."

"Yes, I was. That was a long time ago. It was the last year I worked there. So unfortunate what happened."

"What happened? What do you mean?"

"Oh you know. The baby."

"Baby?" Grace was shocked. No one, absolutely no one in forty years had ever mentioned her pregnancy, or the fact that she missed one half of her sophomore year. She came back, went to summer school, had a tutor, and caught up with her classmates by the middle of her junior year. Everyone always referred to it as the time she had to go and help her relatives. No one ever said "pregnant," or "baby."

"Yes, of course, I knew."

"Why? Why of course?"

"Well, your mother. You know."

"No, I don't know. What are you talking about?"

"Well, maybe now is not the time. Not the place, huh? With your mother passing, I thought we could be more open about it." Patty looked down at the table, moved the silverware, and placed the napkin in her lap. "Maybe not."

"I'm sorry but I have no idea what you're talking about, or insinuating. Please tell me." Grace heard the plea in her voice. She tried to suck it back in. Her vulnerability was stretched to the limit.

"Well, dear, this seems to be stressing you out." Patty looked directly into Grace's eyes. She recognized the pain there.

"Mrs. Perkins, for forty years I have cried over a baby that I loved and was denied. My own parents lied to me, told me the baby didn't exist. Only now, have I found photographs and papers that prove to me that I gave birth to a son and that son was known by my mother but always hidden from me. Tell me what you know. Please."

"Your mother never told you?"

"No. She said the baby died at birth. They wouldn't let me see it, they wouldn't let me know if it was a boy or a girl. If you know something, tell me. Please."

Grace sorted through her purse looking for a tissue, tears rippled down her cheeks. She didn't care, she couldn't stuff it back in anymore. She looked at Patty, the first person who did not deny that there had been a baby. "Please tell me."

The waiter came to the table, "Are you ready to order?" Feeling the intensity between the two women, one in tears, he said, "I'll give you a little more time," and stepped away from the table.

"I think we both have been lied to. I'm so sorry. All this time I was told one thing and you were told something altogether different. It seems a miracle that nothing ever came to light until now."

Grace stared at her. She thought *Please,* but she had already said it so many times. She did not trust her voice to say it again. She wanted to scream at the top of her lungs. The truth felt so close.

"Can you keep your composure? I will tell you. I don't think that this is the right place though. Let's go across the street to my son's office and use his conference room. We can always come back for lunch."

Grace stared. There was something in the back of her mind. In her memory there was something so similar. *What was it? What had happened before? Was it when I left school? Was it later than that?* She had no ability to argue, she was going to follow this woman wherever, to learn the truth.

They walked outside the restaurant and across the street. When they entered the medical office, the receptionist greeted them "Mrs. Perkins, Ms. Steed, Doctor isn't in. Was he expecting you?"

"No dear. We just wanted to use the conference room for a little while. Okay?"

"Sure. Do you want me to bring coffee? Tea? Anything?"

"No, we're fine. Thank you."

Patty Perkins sat down and patted the seat beside her. Grace sat. Despite being fifty-five years old, she felt fifteen again. *That was it! Mrs. Perkins took me aside when I was leaving school. She told me to take good care of myself and the baby. She said, "This is unfortunate, but you will live. You need to keep growing up. You may not know it now, but you are too young."*

Grace looked at Patty. Patty nodded. "You remember something? What do you remember?"

Grace told her. Patty nodded again.

"Many lives will be affected by what I say now. It was never my intention to keep this quiet. But one thing led to another, and there was no way to undo what had been done. Your mother made it easy to just let things remain unspoken."

"Tell me."

"Do the math child. I was fifty-four, your age now, when you became pregnant. My husband and I had been married for thirty years and never had a child. I never even conceived. We were considered too old to adopt by then. Your mother came to me and told me she would take you from school. She wanted you to come back and be put into studies to catch up as quickly as possible. She wanted you to go to college. I asked about the baby. She said it would be put up for adoption. She said it would drain their savings to send you away and pay for the medical care. We reached a bargain. I said I knew a respectable couple that wanted a child. I said they had enough money to pay for the best medical care, and that they could provide for the child.

Grace's breath caught in her throat. She made a choking sound that scared Patty.

"Are you alright?"

Grace nodded.

"Your mother had a lawyer in Mt. Hastings draw up an agreement. You were sent to live with my cousin and her husband. They were to provide for you and to let us know when the baby was coming. Your mother said you didn't want the child, that you had been taken advantage of, raped. She said that you wanted your life back. When I offered to let you see the child, your mother threatened to take him from us. She said that under no circumstances should I say anything. You were never to know that he was growing up right here in Cedar Meadows."

"When he was young we sent photos to her, it was part of the condition of the adoption, but to the best of my knowledge she never saw him, or talked to him. She had us send photos to a post office box. He never met your parents."

"But…" Grace couldn't speak. She sobbed.

Patty pulled her into an embrace and continued. "In those days people didn't show off their "bump" like girls do today. Pregnancy was not talked about in polite company. I retired that year and we moved away for several years. When we came back we had a child. Everyone knew I was older. I was prepared to say that we had adopted, but no one ever asked. After a while it was impossible to bring it up."

"But your son is Corey.... the papers said Jasper."

"I named him after my father and my husband. He was christened Jasper Cornelius Perkins. As his father was Jasper, we called him Corey and it stuck. He doesn't know I know, but when he was in medical school he legally changed his name to Corey Perkins."

Grace continued to sob. Patty took a white linen handkerchief from her purse. It was trimmed with lace. She handed it to Grace. "I am so sorry that I never broached the subject directly with you. I believed your mother. I thought she was protecting you. I was afraid of her, she had the power to take him from me. I feared that she would do it, even when he was old enough that I knew that she could not. I realize how much pain this must have caused you."

Grace blew her nose, sat back and looked at Patty. "What do we do now?"

"What do you want to do?"

"I want to be a part of his life. I don't know other than that. But I don't want to cause any harm."

The door opened. Corey asked in a jovial manner, "What's going on in here?"

Both women turned to see Corey standing there. He looked from one to the other, then rushed to his mother's side.

"Really, what is going on here? Mom, are you okay?" He looked from Grace who was crying to his mother who looked like she had seen a ghost. He took her wrist, taking her pulse. She shook his hand away.

"Sit down Corey."

He took the chair beside her. "Grace, what's going on?"

Grace smiled but still had tears in her eyes. She looked to Patty, she had no idea what to say. This was her son. Suddenly she could see the resemblance. *How could I have missed this? He has my father's nose.* She was overcome with emotion.

Patty reached over and took her son's hand. "I'm an old woman and I don't have that much longer. I have to right a wrong. I'm an old fool, son."

"What are you talking about?"

"I have to tell you something I should have told you when you were a child."

"What?"

"Stop," said Grace. She shook her head at Patty. "Enough."

"No, it's not enough. I owe you a lifetime of happiness."

Whatever are you talking about?" Corey was looking from one to the other. Neither Patty nor Grace spoke.

"Oh!" he said.

"Oh?" Patty said. "What oh?"

"I wondered if this would ever come to light. Are we talking about adoption?"

"Yes," she said. "What do you know?"

"I'm a doctor. In medical school, we take courses in genetics and learn how to type blood. I am a type B and neither you nor dad were B, you were both O. In genetics, we learned about dominance and here I am with brown eyes, and both you and dad had blue eyes. I asked you then about grandparents and their eye color. I remember asking a lot about why I didn't have a brother or a sister when I was young, then I added the age thing and figured I was adopted."

He looked from Patty to Grace. He calculated her age, her eye color. "Are you my mother?"

She nodded and smiled. Her heart melted at the word.

He got up and walked around the table. He put his arms around her and said, "See, I come from good stock."

They sat together for the next hour getting hungrier and hungrier, but they talked about everything that they had to share so each knew what the other knew.

"Doc, sorry to interrupt but the hospital is on line three," the nurse said.

30.

"Susie? It's Velma Batterson. Me and Brick are ready to sell. Call us back."

Susie Johnson played the message three times before she called them back. She wanted to be sure she heard them right, and she wanted to be sure that a full hour passed before she called.

"Velma, its Susie. I got your message. Come on down to the office and sign the offer."

"Then we can still go through with it?"

"Yes. I'll call them right now and let them know you are ready to sign."

"Brick woke up this morning and said I was a silly fool. That he was going to move into town with or without me. So, I guess we are ready to go."

"I'll see you shortly."

Susie leaned back in her chair, threw her pencil up in the air and yelled "Yahoo things are back to normal."

31.

Walt Walters finally got a call from Eleanor.

"Seems I'm as much of an old fool as the mayor," she said. "It scared me to hear that he was in the hospital. Of course things are going to change now. What with a DUI and a suspended license he is gonna' rely on me to get around. You can tear up the paperwork and send me a bill for your time."

As he listened, he looked out across Crescent Street and saw Patty Perkins, Corey Perkins and Grace Steed walking arm in arm from Corey's office to the

Meadow Brook Diner. *Looks like my intuition was right on. They figured it out on their own. This is looking like a good day. Maybe I should call Olivia.*

"Hi Olivia, it's me, Walt."

"Hi Walt, what's up?"

"I'm calling to get an astrology reading today."

"Looks like it has cleared up. Mercury has turned its orbit back toward Earth, the full moon is waning."

"Are you up for a little romance?"

"My planets are aligned for that."

32. Epilogue

"You are going to love living here in Cedar Meadows. The weather is perfect, the people are friendly and there is no traffic. Sometimes we have to make up things to gossip about because life is laid back and quiet," Susie Johnson said to Pete and Paula Crown who were buying the Batterson's farm. "Come on inside. I'm happy to give you the grand tour."

The Writer

The writer sits at her desk, fingers poised over the keys. She gathers her thoughts, but they stray quickly to the dream that woke her. She woke in terror, clammy, her legs twisted in the sheets, the nightmare coming back in waves. Now, hours later, she cannot pull one strand of that dream forward.

It must have been important. Why else was I in such a state? Still nothing. She inspects the fingernails of her right hand. The day-old polish intact, shiny, a sea foam green-blue. Satisfied, she looks over the nails of her left hand, noting that the polish has scuffed off the tip of her forefinger, the ‘F" "R" and T" key tapper. She thinks of herself as a writer, but she is unpublished. She ventured into this career choice when she moved to this house by the sea, left to her by an aunt. It seemed like the perfect setting for a writer.

The tick tick of the minute hand is the only sound in the room, reminding her that time is slipping by. She stares at the page where the character Miranda waits for action. What was the plot? Where was the next turn? What was the dream?

It is her habit to rise early and write. She has written nothing today. She shakes her head and decides to start the day over, and heads to the shower.

Thirty minutes later she returns to the keyboard. It is warm; sunshine illuminates the room. She adjusts the blinds and stares at the blank page. Suddenly the room is intolerably hot; she licks at beads of perspiration on her upper lip. The taste of salt pleases and alarms her. She rises, leans across the desk to open the window. It moves only an inch. She readjusts her feet, leveraging her strength, and hefts the window up. "Owww," she moans as a sharp pain sears her lower back. She lets go of the window, falls forward, her hands on the desk. She holds herself there, pressing upward into her shoulders lifting the strain off her back. Her hands rest uneven on the piles of unfinished stories.

Here is the mystery where Detective Lawrence has cornered the potential killers in the darkened room and waits for the clue that will identify them, there is a love story where the heroine is a mysterious healer who is whispered to be an angel, the science fiction trilogy about colonization, and the faux biography of her relative pioneers in Montana. So many stories, started, left undone. Will she ever have time to finish them and bring the reader to a state of emotional satisfaction?

She pushes herself upright. "Owww," she moans again. She drops to the floor and lays on her back, pressing her lower back to the floor. She lifts her knees to her chest, hands around them and rocks gently from side to side. Is this what the chiropractor told me to do? Has this ever worked? She slowly lowers her legs to the floor. Her back is quiet, no spasm, no pain. She listens to the crash of the waves pounding on the shore. From this house, she cannot see the sea, but she can hear it and smell salt in the morning air. She rolls to her left side and turns onto all fours, then rises. She rests on the couch; sleep overcomes her.

In her study, the afternoon breeze rises, and fresh air wafts gently through the open window, then builds to a breathy pulse. Pages on the desk quiver in the breeze, a page from the love story drifts over and falls onto the mystery. The action adventure, closest to the open window, disperses pages over the stacks and onto the floor. Over the next hour as the writer sleeps, her stories scatter themselves mingling characters and twisting plots.

When she wakes, her back seems healed, and she returns to the study. Pages, scattered across the floor, cover the muted blue-gray Persian carpet. Her hands fly up. This is what woke her in the night. Her stories are unnumbered, no footnotes or headers, no way to discern one page from another, all in Times New Roman twelve point font. She reaches for the light switch, turns on the overhead fan in error and watches in horror as the pages lift and swirl, ten years efforts a flutter.

Made in the USA
Charleston, SC
26 October 2016